MEMORIES OF THE PAST

S.L. STERLING

Memories of the Past

ISBN: 978-1-989566-43-5

Paperback ISBN: 978-1-989566-46-6

Harcover ISBN: 978-1-989566-47-3

Editor: Brandi Aquino, Editing Done Write

Cover Design: Thunderstruck Cover Design

CHAPTER 1

Thomas

June 2009

Trinity sitting across from me, a soft smile on her face, and our favorite small diner, The Crispy Biscuit, had become my favorite way to spend an early Saturday morning. She was beautiful in every single way. I watched as she read the menu, the sunlight bouncing off her blond hair, and I realized that I could not wait for her to be mine. After this summer, our dreams, our plans would come true. As soon as we graduated, we were planning on taking a road trip, and we decided that before we returned to Willow Valley we would be married.

"What are you thinking of having this morning?" I asked, smiling at her.

"Hmmm, I don't know." She tapped her forefinger on her bottom lip. "It's a cross between... pancakes or waffles." We both said the last part in unison, then laughed.

It was one of the many things I loved about Trinity. She was a creature of habit, and every Saturday morning since we started dating in the tenth grade, she had done the exact same thing when we came for breakfast. She would debate between the two items, seeming to find the choice harder than the week before, but each time she would go for the waffles.

She looked back down at the menu, still laughing. "We both already know I will go for the waffles. I don't know why I even bother looking," she said, closing the menu and placing it off to the side.

"I know, but it's fun to watch you crinkle your nose as you sift through the menu, and your eyes light up when you finally decide. If you really want, next Saturday I won't let them give you a menu. Perhaps that way the decision will come easier." I chuckled and winked at her, as she laughed again.

The moment I met her, I knew she was special, and the more I'd gotten to know her, the faster I fell head over heels for her. She took a sip of water and began talking about our upcoming trip and how we would have to find every single waffle house location on our way. Unbeknownst to her, I had already mapped them out, purposefully planning out our trip just so we would hit those locations. Trinity was the love of my life, and there was nothing that I wouldn't do for her.

"Don't you worry. I've got it all taken care of." I winked just as Brooke approached our table to take our order.

"Well, if it isn't the two lovebirds. What will you have this morning? Wait, let me guess, you'll have the waffles, and you will have eggs, bacon, and toast."

"You got it." I answered, reaching across the table and grabbing Trinity's hand. Brooke and Trinity had once been best friends, that was, until Brooke had made a pass at me. I saw Brooke glance down to our hands, then she scribbled down the order, and turned and walk away.

"How's things at home?" Trinity questioned, quietly, so no one could hear.

Things had been strained between my father and me for a few months. He had wanted me to work for him on the ranch this summer and had been making life hard for me since I'd told him I was going to travel. It was something that the occupants of Willow Valley didn't need to know, and I appreciated her keeping her voice low. Gossip had a way of spreading in this town.

I shrugged; I'd hoped she wouldn't bring it up this

morning. It was something that I hadn't wanted to talk about. Instead, I just wanted to spend time with my girl and pretend that everything was fine, but I knew the question came from a caring placing inside Trinity. "Not good. I've worked sunup to sundown almost every day we've been out of school the past two weeks. He just won't let up."

"I'm sorry," Trinity said, looking down at her hands. "I was hoping things would get better."

"I just don't understand why he can't respect my wishes." Instantly, I could feel the tension rising within myself, and since I didn't want to ruin breakfast, I did my best to shrug it off. "Let's not talk about it, okay."

"Okay, we won't talk about it." Trinity grew quiet as she looked off across the street. "Hey, I think there is a man waving at you. Didn't that guy work for your Dad at one point?" Trinity asked.

I looked in the direction she was pointing, and sure enough, Jed Hawkins was stopped at the crosswalk waving in our direction. I raised my hand and waved, Jed waving back. Jed had worked on my father's ranch for a couple of years when I was just a kid, prior to joining the rodeo. He barely made it back to Willow Valley, but when he did, he always stopped in to see my father, and he always took the time to talk to me. He would come into Willow Valley normally with the rodeo.

"Thomas! How are you?" Jed said, approaching our table. "Miss," he said, tilting his hat.

"Good, Jed. What brings you back to Willow Valley?" I questioned, standing up, now meeting his height.

"Ah, you know, same old thing. We're putting on a demonstration down at the Darling Ranch. You should come and check it out later today or tomorrow. You expressed interest the last time I was in town."

"I just might do that," I said, knowing it would piss off my father. I caught Trinity glancing up at me with curiosity.

"Okay then, I won't take up any more of your time, we can catch up later. Enjoy your breakfast with this cutie, and we can catch up later. I'll keep an eye out for you today, but I saw you and wanted to come over."

"Sounds good. It was good seeing you, and I look forward to seeing what you are doing over at Darling Ranch."

As soon as Jed was gone, Brooke brought out our plates of breakfast and placed them in front of us, refilled our coffee, and went to another table. I was about to dig in when I noticed Trinity was still staring at me.

"What is it?"

"Are you really going to go and check things out

over at the Darling Ranch?"

"Ah it's just the rodeo demonstrations that I might go check out." I shrugged as if it were no big deal while shoving a forkful of fried potatoes into my mouth. "Beats dealing with my father."

"I thought you had to work for your dad today?"

"When don't I have work to do for my father," I said under my breath. "If I'm late, so be it. He'll have to deal with it."

Trinity picked up the syrup and poured it over her stack of waffles, then dug her fork into them. "You're not going to do anything stupid are you?" she asked, smiling.

"Like?"

"Oh, I don't know, something along the lines of running away with the western circus?"

I chuckled. "No, Trinity, I'm not," I said, placing my hand on her knee under the table. I didn't want to upset her, but there was nothing wrong with going to see the demonstration. I knew she was worried about things between my father and me. She expressed her feelings numerous times over the past few weeks. She also knew how my father could be and how he may react to my being late. He was already strict enough without provoking him. "It will be fine," I assured her. "Now eat up, before they get cold."

Once breakfast was over, I walked Trintiy back to

the small apartment that she shared with her aunt, which sat above Bluebird Books, her aunt's bookstore. We stopped in front of the small bookstore and watched her Aunt Vi through the window, dealing with a customer. It took a moment before she waved at us. Trinity and I smiled and waved back, and then she turned to me.

"Will I see you tonight for the movie in the park?" she questioned, looking up at me with her big beautiful blue eyes.

"Of course. I'll pick you up at the usual time." I pulled her into me for a hug and felt her arms wrap around me. She rested her cheek against my chest, and I closed my eyes, relishing in the scent of her perfume and the fact that her body fit so well against mine. As she pulled away, I placed my hand on her cheek and met her lips, kissing her softly. "See you tonight," I whispered, kissing her lips again before she left me standing there.

I stood against the fence at Darling Ranch, watching as men from all over Willow Valley tried out for the rodeo.

"Thomas, you decided to come after all," I heard Jed's gruff voice from behind me.

I turned to see Jed standing behind me, a smile on his face. "Hey, Jed, figured I'd come down and see what it was all about before I made my way back home. What I've seen so far looks pretty interesting."

"Sure is. I've loved it since I left. Did you want to try out?" Jed asked, coming to stand beside me.

I glanced to the ring to see my good friend John holding on for dear life as the bull he was on bucked away.

"I don't know," I said, my voice full of hesitation. How would I explain an injury to Trinity, or to my father. Trinity just thought I'd come purely out of curiosity, and my father didn't have a clue I was even here. In fact, I had been halfway home before I turned around and made my way to the Darling Ranch.

"What's stopping you?" Jed questioned. "There is nothing wrong with trying out. Besides, I don't think you want to stay in Willow Valley forever."

Jed had left Willow Valley almost ten years ago and had a very good career up to this point. I'd followed his career closely; he was, after all, one of the guys who'd worked on my father's ranch, one of the only ones who paid me any attention. So, I was genuinely curious to see how he'd made out. He'd left and done very well for himself.

"No, I don't want to spend the rest of my life in Willow Valley. As a matter of fact, I'm itching to get the hell out of here."

"Well then? Just give it a try. In this career, you'll get to travel the world. See amazing places."

"I know. It's just Trinity and I have plans. We are going to spend our summer traveling, then at the end of the summer, before we return, we are going to get married."

"Well then, it's the perfect time. Bring Trinity with you. The rodeo needs some fresh blood. I'll get your name on the list. I've seen you ride. You've got promise, Thomas."

"You've seen me ride a horse." I chuckled. "Besides, my dad will kill me."

"Your father won't even know. You're simply trying out, not leaving with us tonight." Jed turned and walked over to a man with a clipboard, spoke with him, then they both turned and looked at me. He scribbled something down on the clipboard; Jed smacked him on the back and walked back over to me. "All set. Eleven thirty, be at the opening of the chute. I'll get you all set."

I returned home shortly after two. Immediately, I made my way out to the barn in a rush to find my dad. I knew he would be angry. I was late, but I was so excited to tell him about the tryouts.

I checked the first barn only to find it empty, then I stepped into the second barn to find my father and two ranch hands down on the ground dealing with what appeared to be a very sick calf. The second he laid eyes on me he barked, "Where the hell you been?"

I was about to tell him about the tryouts when he held his hand up. "You know what, Thomas, never mind. You're here now, and you've got work to do. The stalls in the main barn need cleaning. You also need to get the horses watered and fed."

I looked at my father. "But, Dad, I have—"

"Whatever it is can wait. The horses can't, nor can the stalls. You're behind on your chores. Had you of been in here this morning like you were supposed to have been, I probably would have been alerted to this sick calf well before now. Instead, I was busy tending to all the things you do."

I glanced down to the sick calf that lay on the floor in distress, while Billy and Lyle glanced up at me, neither of them saying anything.

"What's wrong with her?" I questioned.

"Does it really concern you? No, what does concern you is those horses. Now get into that barn and get the stalls cleaned, and those horses fed and watered. Oh, and you're mother wants you to grab some strawberries from the garden for dessert. She's busy with the church bazaar today." He turned around and knelt back down giving Lyle instructions that I could barely hear.

I stood there watching as Lyle got up and left the barn, going to get whatever my father had told him to, then my father looked over his shoulder at me. "I thought I told you to get to the stalls," he barked. "I don't have time to argue with you right now."

I let out a huff, looked at Billie, then turned away from my father, making my way to the other barn to begin cleaning out stalls. There was no point in trying to talk to him when he was angry.

I kicked a stone as I made my way to the barn, pissed that he hadn't given me a chance to talk to him. I don't know why it surprised me; he never took the time to hear me. He'd basically blamed me for everything and turned his back on me. As always, everything was more important than anything I ever had to tell him. I approached the barn door and pulled it open and made my way over to the first stall and began cleaning it out. Some of the other ranch hands were already working away on some of the stalls that I was supposed to clean, each of them glancing my way, pissed that they had been forced to take on more work.

I just put my head down and went about the job at hand, forgetting that they were there.

Three hours later, I was finished with everything that my father had asked me to do. I'd had long enough to think over things, so I made my way up to the house and to my room. I hadn't been able to get the tryouts out of my mind, nor the things Jed had said about getting to see the world. I showered, and then, as if forced by someone else's hand, I returned to my room, dressed, and began packing a bag. I'd made up my mind. I was leaving in the morning with Jed, and I would take Trinity with me.

I walked out the front door, bag in hand, and threw it into the back of my truck. I glanced in the direction of the main barn and could hear my father still barking orders at the others. He was on a roll today, and Mom still wasn't back yet. There was no way I was going to bother even attempting to tell him I was leaving, so I climbed into the front seat of my beat-up old truck and turned the key, the old engine sputtering to life.

I began pulling down the driveway as my mother's car came up the drive. I was instantly reminded about the strawberries I'd forgotten to pick and knew that once I returned home for the night, my father would have more words to spew at me. Instead of worrying about it, I cranked the radio and continued down the driveway.

I pulled onto Bluebird Lane and stopped right out front of Bluebird Books, cutting the engine. I rested my arm on the window ledge and sat waiting for Trinity. It was a little after seven thirty, the closed sign hung in the window of her aunt's bookstore, and I could see Trinity talking with her through the window.

My stomach hurt as I tried to come up with an idea of how I was going to tell her that I was leaving for the rodeo, and how I was going to ask her to come with me. I knew she would understand; she had to. She and I would go, see all the cities and small towns, and the best part was that we would experience them together —if she wanted. I hoped she wanted to. I heard the jingle of the little bell that hung above the bookstore door, and Trinity came walking out, her small clutch purse in her hand. She was wearing my favorite yellow sunflower sundress, and she smiled as her long blond hair waved in the wind.

Instantly, a lump formed in my throat as my stomach turned. I wanted more for us than I had realized, and more than this town had to offer us, and there was nothing that was going to stop me.

CHAPTER 2

Trinity

I leaned against the old wooden counter of Bluebird Books waiting for Thomas to arrive. The smell of wood and books hung in the air as I listened to my aunt talk about the upcoming sale she'd been planning for a month.

"I'm going to need you here, Trin. There is just too much to do and without Becky. She won't be able to work until her ankle heals. Poor girl, there couldn't have been more of an inconvenient time for her to break her ankle, what with it being summer and all."

"I know, Aunt Vi. I'll do whatever I can up until the time I leave." I shrugged, seeing Thomas pull up and stop his truck right outside the large picture window.

"Unfortunately, Trinity, I don't think I can have you leave even for a week at this point. I'm swamped here. You know more people are out and about in the summer. Plus, I have not only this sale, but in two week's time the street fair is on. You know what kind of business that brings in here. Tourists from all over stop here. Then there is maintaining the gardens, and laundry, cleaning the apartment. It will be too much for me."

I swallowed hard. "But what about my trip with Thomas?" I cried, tears filling my eyes. "We've been planning it for months."

"I know, dear. Perhaps you can reschedule it for the fall, or late summer, once Becky is back. I know Thomas is needed on the ranch as well. Betty was in the other day. She told me that William has a lot of plans this summer, but I'm sure his father has already told him. That's a big operation they have going there. I'd imagine it takes all hands to make it run. Besides, I know that he wants to groom Thomas to take over the ranch once they are ready to retire."

Disappointment filled me. There was no point in talking to Aunt Vi about Thomas's father and how horrible he had been to Thomas over the last few months. Nor was there any point in talking back to her. If she needed my help, then I would talk to Thomas and see if we could postpone our trip for a few weeks. He would understand, I knew he would. It would also give him time to hopefully work things out with his father.

I glanced out the front window to see Thomas's truck and reached for my clutch bag and walked over to my aunt, placing a kiss on her cheek. "I'll talk to Thomas," I said reluctantly. "I will explain everything and see if we can't make it work. I'll make sure I'm here to help you."

"Thank you, Pet. You always were a good girl. Have a good time tonight and don't be out too late. I'll leave the back door open."

"I will, and I won't be too late. Oh, and you don't need to leave the door open. I have my key," I sang and then giggled as I shoved open the door, stepping out onto the sidewalk, excited to spend the night with Thomas. I could see him watching me from the driver's seat as I approached his truck, a soft smile on his lips.

"Sorry about that," I said as I climbed into the truck, placing my purse by my feet, "Aunt Vi was having a mini breakdown in there." I leaned over the console and meeting his lips.

"Another one?" Thomas chuckled as he put his

truck into gear and gently pulled out onto the road in the direction of the park. Movies Under the Stars was one of our favorite events of the summer. Every Saturday night, the local theater owner ran this event. We hadn't missed one since we'd been dating.

"What movie is playing tonight?" I questioned.

"I think it's *Knowing*, with Nicholas Cage. Supposed to be good."

The crowd was already building as Thomas pulled into the parking lot and cut his engine. I glanced into the back seat, my eyes falling to the duffle bag that sat there. Thomas reached around and grabbed the large blanket we always used, and I averted my eyes and said nothing about the bag.

We walked across the field, hand-in-hand, until we were in our usual area, and together, we spread out the blanket, then I sat down while he went over to the small refreshment table to grab a couple of drinks and a large bag of popcorn.

The longer I watched him, the more curious I became of the duffel bag sitting on the back seat of his car. It hadn't been there last night. In fact, it had never been there this morning either, and it looked full.

"Here you go, Trin." He held out the small pop for me to take. I grabbed both drinks and placed them down, while he sat down next to me. He leaned over and gently kissed me, his tongue washing through my mouth.

"So, how was your day?" I asked, as our lips parted.

Thomas shrugged. "I went down to check out the rodeo tryouts this morning," he said in a low voice.

"What for? I thought you said you weren't going to go."

"I never said I wouldn't go. Besides, I was curious. Plus, it was nice to spend some time with Jed. He always made time for me when I was younger."

I grew quiet. I had no idea why Thomas had gone to those tryouts, but I feared it had something to do with his home situation at this moment. The last little bit he had done nothing but talk about us leaving and getting a place of our own.

"You do know I can't elope until I turn eighteen right," I said, placing my hand on his strong forearm.

Thomas paused and looked at me. "Where is that coming from?"

I gave him a knowing look and a gentle smile. "I saw the bag." I giggled. "It has to be at the end of summer."

His face went pale, and I could see the muscles in his throat tense. "Ah, yeah, about that…"

Something was wrong, I could tell. "What about it?"

He turned his eyes away from me. "I'm…oh God, how do I even say it," he murmured more to himself than to me.

"You just say it," I said, placing my hand on his and lacing my small fingers through his. "We've always been up front with one another."

Thomas looked at me, his eyes growing dark. "Trin, I've decided to join the rodeo."

"What?" I asked, shocked, not believing what I was hearing.

Thomas took in a deep breath and looked away from me. Then he sighed. "I don't know, Trin. My father made me angry today. He gets mad at every little thing I do or don't do. There is no making him happy, and I guess I just want out from under his thumb and have some sort of an adventure before I settle down."

Tension filled my body at his words. I tried hard not to focus on the last three words he had spoken. "More adventure than the ranch?" I asked.

"Yeah, I don't want to spend the summer working like a dog under my father's thumb. That much I can say. He was pissed earlier today when I finally returned to the ranch. He came down on me hard right in front of the ranch hands. Granted, he was dealing with a sick calf, but the way he did it, those guys would never respect me now, nor will they ever after the way he tore me up. I can only imagine how much disrespect they would have for me if I were the one in charge of that ranch."

I didn't know what to say. I knew Mr. Jenkins could be rough at times—I'd seen it—but I also didn't think he would tear Thomas up like that, especially in front of his employees. He knew how important it was that they respected Thomas.

"Perhaps you just need to have a talk with your father, explain to him how you feel."

"My father doesn't work that way and you know it. Showing feelings is to show weakness."

"Thomas...."

"You could come with me, you know. Travel the world with me, see places that, well, that we would probably never get to see otherwise," Thomas said, ignoring my suggestion.

Instantly, I thought about Aunt Vi and how she'd practically been in tears today when Becky had called to tell us she'd broken her ankle after she slipped on the stairs at home. I already knew that there wasn't a way I could abandon her now.

"When are you planning on leaving?" I asked, my voice low.

"Jed told me that they were pulling out of town

tomorrow night. He said he can give me a job until I get on my feet. He'd even let me ride his bulls and enter some events if I gave him ten percent of my earnings."

My stomach dropped at the news. I could tell he was serious. "What about our trip?"

"Well, I thought about that. Instead of taking the trip we'd planned, this will be our trip. We'll go and see all the sights, more than what we would ever see just traveling together, until the end of summer. I can earn some money, and once we've saved up enough, I'll get us a small place. It probably won't be much at first, but I'm a hard worker. I'll make sure you won't want for anything."

I listened as he spoke. I still hadn't even mentioned the fact that Aunt Vi would need me over most of the summer and that I wouldn't be able to go on the trip anyway. I didn't really need to. It appeared to me that Thomas had made up his mind, and it wouldn't matter what I said anyway. He was planning on leaving with Jed in the morning for the silly promises that the rodeo life could offer. I wondered if he'd even mentioned any of this to his mother. Did they even know? I sucked in a deep breath, about to ask him, when the opening credits to the movie began to play.

Thomas leaned back on his elbows as he always did

and turned his attention to the screen, while tears stung my eyes. I was ready to leave to head back home and put my head in my pillow. When I didn't lean back and rest against him, he placed his hand on my shoulder and tapped his chest, telling me to relax back on him.

I shook my head; I knew that if I rested my body against his, I would crumble into a million pieces. The hurt I felt was almost too much to bear, so I just sat there staring at the screen, wishing it was over.

"You're really quiet," he whispered, his lips grazing my ear as he leaned into me halfway through the movie.

I wanted to lash out at him and tell him he was being selfish, but I didn't. Instead, I just shrugged. "There really isn't much to say, now is there."

Thomas looked at me, hurt in his eyes. "Sure there is. Tell me what you're thinking, Trin. We always talk about things and work through them together," he whispered, trying not to disturb the others who were around us.

I stared at the movie screen, biting my tongue, weighing my words before I spoke.

"You can come with me, like I said. I want you to come with me. I want you by my side, forever," he said, wrapping his arms around me.

The more he spoke, the more upset I became, until I couldn't take it anymore. "I can't go with you, Thomas. As a matter of fact, I can't go with you on our planned trip either. Aunt Vi needs my help this summer. She's asked me to see if we could hold off until the fall."

Thomas slowly let me go and looked at the ground, a look of unease on his face.

"She's done so much for me since Mamma passed away. I couldn't stand to see her cry this afternoon, so as much as I don't understand this need you have to go join the rodeo circuit, I also need you to understand that leaving is not something I can do right now."

"I do understand. I understand completely, but it still doesn't stop the fact I want you with me. Perhaps you can meet up with me the end of summer or in the fall, if you still want to," he said, laying back and pulling a brochure from his back pocket.

"What's that?"

"The schedule. This has every stop we'll be making, so, when I get to August, I'll be..." He opened the brochure and quickly ran his finger down the list of city names.

It didn't matter that I couldn't go. He was still going to leave me. I swallowed the hard lump that had formed in my throat at his words, 'if I wanted,' and placed my hand over his, stopping him. “Thomas, can you just take me home?” I pleaded.

He looked up from the paper he held in his hand and met my eyes, studying them.

“Please, Thomas, take me home.”

He didn’t say anything. He just sat there looking at me until I could no longer meet his eyes. When we finally broke eye contact, he began folding the brochure back up, sliding it into his shirt pocket, then he picked up his drink and the untouched popcorn container without saying a word to me and carried them to the garbage. I didn’t move, and when he returned, he looked down at me. “Well, if you want to go, let’s go.”

Thomas pulled up to the curb, and I could see out of my peripheral that he turned to look at me. I didn’t turn to meet his eyes. Instead, I sat staring forward, unsure of what was to come next. He pulled the brochure out of his pocket and held it out for me to take. I glanced at the crinkled paper.

“Like I said, I’d like you with me in August. If you want to come, that is.”

There it was again, those words. *If I wanted.* I swallowed hard and ripped the brochure from him. Then without as much as a good-bye, I climbed out of the truck and watched from the sidewalk as Thomas pulled away from the curb. He never even gave so much as a backward glance. I took in a deep breath, the smell of gardenias in the fresh night air. I prayed that tomorrow would somehow be different, that he'd think twice and come back to me, even though I knew deep down that nothing would change. I turned around and looked at my aunt's small bookshop, the storefront dark, but the lights in our second-floor apartment were on. I made my way into the side yard and went to the back door, sliding my key into the lock.

I climbed the back stairs up to the apartment and placed my shoes on the small pink mat at the top of the stairs. I glanced into the living room to see Aunt Vi, in her favorite chair, a crossword book in hand as she looked at me over the rim of her glasses.

"Trinity? You're back early. Goodness, it is barely even nine thirty?"

I nodded, unable to speak because I knew my voice would shake and the tears would fall.

"Is everything okay?" she questioned, setting her book to the side and leaning forward, a concerned look on her face.

Instead of answering her, I threw the brochure

down on the floor and made a dash to my room, flopping down on my bed and crying into my pillow. The lump that had been in my throat most of the night was now even bigger than before, and I could barely swallow as I cried.

I felt the bed lower and my aunt's hand on rest on my back. "It's okay, Trinity," she whispered. "What happened?"

How could it be okay? She didn't even know what had gone on. I swallowed hard and caught my breath, then looked off in the opposite direction. "Thomas is leaving for the rodeo." I sobbed. "He didn't even care about what I thought. We're over."

My aunt was silent while I continued to cry my heart out. After a while, she ran her fingers through my hair, pulling the strands out of my face. "I saw the brochure, Pet," she whispered. "I'm sorry, Trinity, but I promise you, dear, you are going to be okay. Men don't think about our feelings."

I frowned; this wasn't how this was supposed to be. I remembered how my father treated my mother, and it was nothing like this. Although I was only a little girl then and probably didn't see it or even know what to look for.

Aunt Vi sat with me for almost an hour, while I continued to cry. She did her best to comfort me, even brought me a cup of warm milk before she went off to bed. Only I couldn't sleep. I lay in bed, staring up at the moon through my window. I'd calmed down and was now quiet. The tears had stopped flowing, and I'd calmed down considerably, yet the hurt and anger still lingered. I let out a breath and rolled onto my back, staring up at the ceiling. The more I thought about what he had said, about the fact that he didn't care that I could leave with him right now, the angrier I got, and once again the tears fell, only this time they didn't stop until I'd cried myself to sleep.

The next morning, I woke. My eyes burned and my chest hurt, and I just wanted to lay in bed, but Aunt Vi forced me up and out of bed. She forced me to eat breakfast, and once she had gone down to open the store, I quietly called Thomas, only to be told that he wasn't home, which started the tears all over again. Had he really gone? His mother didn't sound upset on the phone, so I figured perhaps he was just out working with his father. Only he wasn't. A few hours later his mother had come into the store, and I overheard her speaking with Aunt Vi. She was crying as she spoke, Thomas had joined Jed.

Tears fell for weeks, and then one October morning it was as if someone lifted all the hurt and anger off me and a sense of peace fell over me. I made my way into the small bookstore with a bag of groceries and almost ran into Aunt Vi coming out of the small washroom.

"Oh, Pet, you scared me. You doing okay?" she asked.

"You know what, Aunt Vi?"

"What, dear?"

"You're right. I will be okay," I whispered. I would be okay because in those moments that I'd laid in bed at night, crying and thinking, I'd accepted the fact that Thomas was moving on, and I knew that was what I had to do as well. If he had truly cared about what I'd thought, he wouldn't have left. I sniffled and looked over at her. "I'm a tough cookie."

"I agree, you are. I didn't raise you to be anything but."

It was that exact moment that I decided I would never let another man ever make me feel this way again. That winter, I did what I could to put Thomas out of my mind. It took longer than I expected, and some days, especially at Christmas, were way harder than others. Once people found out Thomas was gone, the girls I'd gone to school with tried hard to set me up with other boys, but I was focused only on the future, learning everything I could about our small bookstore business. In February, I started taking small business classes at a small college just outside of Willow Valley. What my future would bring, I didn't know, but as each day passed, I became more and more excited for it, and by the following fall, Thomas was barely even a thought.

CHAPTER 3

Thomas
August 2022

I lay in the dirt, looking up at a fuzzy, cloudy sky, and blinked hard while trying to catch my breath. The world was completely out of focus, and the harder I tried to bring it back into focus, the dizzier I became. I rubbed my eyes, blinked hard, and then felt two hands grab my arms, and before I knew what had happened, I was up on my feet. I closed my eyes and opened them. the damn bull that had bucked me off. I could see the outline of him, and I blinked again, this time bringing him into sight.

"Come on, Thomas, you need to see the doc," I heard a familiar voice say. It took me a minute to realize it was Aaron.

"I'm fine, Aaron," I mumbled as I stumbled forward.

"The hell you are. That's the fifth time this month you've been thrown, the fourth you've hit your head. you can't take any more risks."

"I said I'm fine." I pulled myself out of Aaron's hold only to fall forward. I was about to brace myself when I felt Aaron grab hold of me.

"Don't tell me you're fine when I know damn well you're not. You can't even stand on your own two feet. Now, we are going to see the doc," Aaron said, directing me toward the gate.

"Fuck, Aaron, I can do it. just let me try once more. Let me get on him once more."

Only Aaron didn't listen. he didn't let me go and try to get back on the bull. Instead, he took me to his truck, got me in the front seat, and then tore off into town to the small hospital.

Five hours later, I sat in the exam room, waiting for the doctor to come back. I'd had a bunch of tests, a couple of scans, and now I sat on the chair waiting for the results. My head ached, so I reached up and turned the lights off, my pounding head instantly calming to a more manageable level. I'd leaned back against the chair and closed my eyes just as the door to the exam room opened.

"Well, doc? What's the news?" I asked. I needed answers. I needed to get back out there onto that bull.

"Thomas, did you turn off the lights?" he asked, frowning at me and looking at me with concern. "I swear I left them on when I left you in here"

"Yeah, my head's been pounding something fierce. It just helps take the edge off."

"I see. Well then, I won't turn them back on." Instead, he turned his small desk lamp on and sat down behind his desk, clasping his hands in front of him, and looked at me. The look on his face already told me the news wasn't good.

"What is it?" I questioned, not sure I was ready to hear the worst.

"How often are you getting these headaches?"

"Oh, I dunno," I lied. "I barely keep track." There wasn't a time in the past few weeks that I remembered not having a headache. I'd gone through all of the medication he'd prescribed for them too.

"Would you say it's more often than before?"

"Hell, doc, I don't know." I shrugged.

"Well, before you said you were getting them two to three times a week. I gave you enough medication for six months. That was two months ago. How much would you say you had left?" he asked, twirling his pen between his fingers, studying me.

I met his eyes; I needed this medication there was no doubt about it. I let out a breath, "Okay fine, I'm getting them four to five times per week. Sometimes, every day," I grumbled. "And I'm out of that medication.

"I see. So, they are all this bad then?" he questioned, making notes in my chart. "So bad that you have to turn off the lights?"

"I wouldn't say that. Some are just worse than others. This is one of the worse than others." I shrugged.

He sat there scribbling down some notes and then looked up at me. "Would you say it's worse when you ride?"

I didn't want to admit it to myself, never mind him, but I nodded. They'd also become worse in the last month, but I wasn't telling him that. "Yeah, sometimes."

He opened the folder in front of him and looked down at the papers in front of him, shuffled a couple of them around, and read the one he'd placed on top. Then he looked up and met my eyes. "Well, Thomas, I'm afraid I have some bad news."

I didn't say anything. I just sat waiting to hear what he was going to say.

"I'm afraid that you are going to have to quit riding."

I shook my head. I couldn't quit. Rodeo was all I knew.

"Thomas, you've had seven concussions in the past year and a half. I told you one more head injury and I'd pull you. I should have done it months ago. Besides, you've got spinal injuries, neck injuries, and with each additional accident, they are getting worse. Each time you get bucked off a bull, you run the risk of being paralyzed. You've got a small pharmacy of pills you've been prescribed in the last year and a half, and it will only continue to get worse, unless you stop. Now, have you been taking all of the medication as prescribed?"

I looked down to the floor. I'd probably been taking more than I'd been prescribed. I nodded. "I doubt I'd be standing if I wasn't taking them." I chuckled.

"Thomas, you've got to stop riding. I'm sorry, but your days of rodeo are over. Here is another prescription to help with those headaches. You're only to take them when your headaches get this bad. I'm going to put a watch on your other scripts as well, make sure you aren't taking too much." He held out a prescription for me to take. "Lucky for you, this time there is no sign of concussion or any more damage to your back or neck."

"Thanks, doc," I muttered and took the small

square of paper and shoved it deep into my pocket, then pulled the door open and made my way down the hall.

The shrill ring of the phone pulled me from a deep sleep. I reached from the bed without opening my eyes, trying to find the phone. Instead, my hand hit something, and I heard the sound of pills and bottles hitting the floor. I glanced at the clock, the fuzzy green numbers slowly coming into focus. It looked to be only a little past six. Who the hell calls someone that early in the morning?

On a normal day, I would have been up by now, but the last few days I'd been sleeping in. I reached for my glasses, my back aching at the stretch. Then I grabbed the only pill bottle still standing and shook two pain pills into the palm of my hand. I grabbed my glass of water, shoved the pills in my mouth, and drank. I looked to the floor at the hundreds of tiny pills that were now scattered all over the floor, then I grabbed the phone, thankful that the noise had finally stopped.

"What is it?" I barked into the phone, pinching my

brow between my thumb and forefinger to take my mind from the headache that had just started.

"Is this Thomas Jenkins?" a woman's voice poured over the phone.

"Yep, who's this?"

"Thomas, are you the son of William and Betty Jenkins, the owners of Jenkins Ranch, in Willow Valley?"

I frowned, wondering what this was about. "I am. Who is this? What's this regarding?"

"Mr. Jenkins, it's Haley Thomas, with Willow Valley Law. You don't know me, but I work with Carson Kinley, your father's attorney. Carson asked me to give you a call. Unfortunately, I have some bad news. Your father passed away on Friday."

I swallowed hard. Mom had passed away a few years ago, and that had been the last time I'd been home. I'd ridden into town and shown up for the funeral, which had been nothing but a mistake. My father wouldn't even look at me, let alone speak to me. I'd stayed for the funeral watching from a distance and I left town the following morning, never once looking back.

"I see," I muttered, dropping my head into my hands.

"Thomas, Carson asked me to arrange a meeting with you in the coming days. There are some things that require attention, and he would like to go over them with you."

"What sort of things?" I questioned, unsure as to what they could possibly need from me.

"Well, Carson has an entire list of things that he actually needs to go over: their bank accounts, investments, what you'd like to do with the ranch."

"The ranch?" I questioned. "Why on earth would he want to know what I want to do with the ranch for?"

"Because according to the will, you now own it."

I ran my hand through my hair and blinked hard. What on earth was this woman talking about. There was no way on God's green earth my father would have left that ranch to me. She had to be mistaken. "I'm sorry, but I don't understand. My father and I didn't exactly see eye to eye on things – or anything for that fact."

"Honestly, Mr. Jenkins, it's probably best that we set up a time that you can meet with Carson once you are back in Willow Valley. Now, when are you planning to come into town?"

I hadn't planned to ever set foot in Willow Valley again. I glanced around my messy loft and ran my hand through my disheveled hair, a million thoughts running through my mind.

"Do you think you could be in town, say Friday morning by nine?"

I had no idea what was going on this week. Actually, that wasn't true, I knew exactly what was going on this week. I was just in denial about not being able to participate. I hadn't mentioned anything to anyone about not being able to ride anymore. I shrugged. "I guess I could be."

"Okay then. Carson has some availability Friday afternoon at three. That should give you plenty of time to stop into the funeral home and confirm the arrangements."

"No one else has done that yet?" I questioned.

"No, sir. Carson figured you'd want to handle that yourself."

I swallowed hard, unsure what to even say to this woman. I just focused on the tiny pills scattered all over the floor and focused on breathing.

"Thomas, are you there?"

"Yeah, yeah I'm here. Three on Friday. I'll see you then." I reached over and placed the phone down, and fell back onto my bed, staring up at the ceiling, trying to accept the news about my father, and the fact that I'd have to return to what used to be home. As I lay there, a tear rolled down my cheek, followed by another as the realization hit that I'd never see my father again. It shouldn't have bothered me. In fact, I didn't understand why it was, so I rolled over on my bed and just lay there, thinking about him.

It was a little past eight when I finally rolled out of bed and reached for my pants. I sat up on the side of the bed and slipped my feet into the legs. I sat there for a moment before reaching for my shirt and throwing it over my head, my back and neck aching with every move. Then I carefully knelt and collected as many pills as I could find, placing them in the empty bottle and securing the lid, while picking up the other closed bottles that had fallen in my panic to silence the phone. I hadn't told Aaron the news from the doctor yet. I'd been to upset when I got home, and I knew he'd never hear anything about my father.

I looked around at the mess of my loft. It wouldn't take me long to pack. I owned nothing but the clothes on my back. I'd packed light since I'd left home all those years ago. Everything else that I had here was courtesy of Aaron. We'd met through the rodeo circuit and had become close. He'd been good to me over the years, and when I became the Triple Crown winner in 2017, I'd tucked away a tiny nest egg for myself and gave him and Amanda the money to purchase this ranch outright. It was the least I could do for all the support he'd given me over the years. In turn, he gave me a roof over my head, food in my stomach, and a decent paying job.

I walked up the back staircase and into the small kitchen off the main house and greeted Aaron's wife, Amanda. She stood at the stove, cooking up scrambled eggs and bacon, the smell of fresh coffee floating in the air.

"Morning, Thomas. Eggs, bacon for you this morning?" she questioned, while pouring me a cup of coffee.

"Please. Is Aaron around?"

"He's out in the barn feeding the horses. He should be up in about five minutes. Why don't you sit down." She nodded to one of the seats at the table and held out the cup for me to take. I was sure Aaron had told her about the bull bucking me off the other night.

"I'll be a minute." I looked out the back door in time to see Aaron step out of the barn. I set the cup on the table and headed out the back door in his direction.

"Morning. How are you feeling? Are ready for another day?" Aaron asked with a smile as I approached him.

"I need to talk to you. I'm afraid I won't be staying.

I, um, got some bad news this morning. My father passed away. I've got to head back to Willow Valley, take care of a few things."

Aaron stopped in his tracks and looked at me. "Thomas, I'm sorry for the loss of your father."

I shrugged, not knowing what to say. Aaron knew we weren't close to one another and hadn't been for some time.

"Thanks."

"What about the weekend?" he questioned.

"What about it?"

"You're supposed to be riding? Have you let them know you won't be there?"

"Yeah, about that. It's almost as if life has finally caught up to me."

"What do you mean?" Aaron asked, looking at me curiously. He'd asked me a couple of times on the way home from the hospital the other night what the doctor had said, but I just kept saying I didn't want to talk about it.

"Doc won't let me ride anymore, Aaron. Too many back and neck injuries. So, unfortunately, it appears that I've ridden my last ride."

Aaron knew all about injuries. He himself had been injured bad a few years back and had to quit as well. "I'm sorry, Thomas. I know how much you love it. So, what are you going to do?"

I leaned against the fence and looked across the fields that surrounded the ranch. It was a scene I had grown to love over the years. There was something so peaceful about it. "I'm not sure yet. Apparently, my father left his ranch to me. So, I'm going to head back, see what shape it's in, and figure it out from there."

Aaron looked to the ground, saddened by what I had told him. "Well, Thomas, please know that you always have a place here, if things don't work out for you. In the meantime, I guess I'll need to start looking for someone to replace you. At least temporarily."

"Thanks. I appreciate that. It feels good knowing that I have somewhere to go if things don't work out."

"Of course, you are always welcome here. Now, I'm sure Amanda has breakfast just about ready. When do you plan on heading out?"

"Later tonight or tomorrow morning at the latest."

"All right, well, let's head up to the house and eat shall we."

"Sounds good."

As I walked beside Aaron, away from the barn, I realized this would be one of the last times I would made this walk. I looked out across the fields, took a deep breath of the fresh air, and realized that I'd really miss this place.

"Breakfast is ready," Amanda called from the back

door, a smile on her face as she watched the two of us approach the house.

Aaron had been lucky to find Amanda, and for the first time in years, I thought about what life would have been like if I'd of stayed in Willow Valley. I wondered what would have happened between Trinity and me. Would we have gotten married and had children? Would we be running Jenkins Ranch now, or would we have gone on and made a life of our own? Though as quickly as those questions entered my mind, I swept those thoughts away.

CHAPTER 4

Trinity

Dark storm clouds hung low in the sky. I sat on the edge of my bed, looking out the window. They said it was going to storm today. I stretched, let out a yawn, and slid my feet into my fuzzy slippers. I wasn't ready to get up yet and wished that it was Sunday, my day off. I grabbed my robe and threw it over my shoulders and looked at my bedside clock. It was only a little after six. I had a little over an hour to get ready for the day and get the store opened.

I opened my bedroom door, expecting to see Aunt Vi in the kitchen cooking up some bacon and eggs, but the apartment was still dark, and her bedroom was closed. I frowned. For as long as I could remember, Aunt Vi was always up before me. Though I'd noticed over the last couple of months that she seemed to be slowing down. Normally, she'd always open the store, but for the last little while I'd been the one to open the shop. Some days she didn't even set foot inside the bookstore, but she always greeted me in the morning.

I listened at her door for a minute. It was quiet, so I went into the kitchen and opened the blinds above the sink. The sun was trying to peek through the clouds to no avail. The kitchen went dark again. I flipped the light on over the sink and turned the kettle on, scooping three teaspoons of coffee grounds into the French press. I went to grab the cream out of the fridge when I felt Luna, my cat, rub up against my legs with a loud purr. I bent down and picked up the tortoiseshell-colored cat and kissed her head. "I guess you want some breakfast, hmmm."

Her loud meow confirmed what I'd asked, and I placed her down on the floor and opened the fridge, pulling out the can of food, and scooped the remainder into her bowl. I placed the bowl onto the floor and watched as she attacked it. I smiled to myself, then turned my attention back to the coffee. Once the two mugs had been filled and were on the small dining room table, I walked over to Aunt Vi's bedroom door and gently knocked.

"Come in, Pet," I heard her soft voice call.

I smiled and opened the door to see Aunt Vi sitting in her favorite recliner, the needlepoint she'd been working on for the past month resting on her lap as she looked over the instructions. "Morning, Aunt Vi. I'm just making some coffee and was about to get breakfast going. Are you hungry?"

"Oh that sounds wonderful, dear. Let me just try and finish up this section. It's giving me some trouble, and I will be right out." She smiled before focusing back on her needlepoint.

I stood in her doorway for a moment. She still wore her favorite pink terrycloth robe over her light-blue pajamas, and her hair was still wild from sleep. Normally, the second she was up, she'd have her hair brushed and tied back and she'd get dressed. I watched her studying her directions, and I suddenly began to worry that she may not be feeling all that well. She looked smaller, a little pale, and I had noticed that lately she was complaining more of aches and pains than ever before.

"Is something wrong, dear?" she asked, not looking up.

"No, it's nothing. I'll go get breakfast," I muttered

and pulled her door shut, heading into my bedroom to get dressed.

I'd just cracked two eggs into the frypan when I heard Aunt Vi behind me. "No eggs for me, dear. I think I'll just have my apple cinnamon oatmeal this morning."

"Oh," I said, wiping my hands on the towel that sat beside the stove. "Okay, let me grab a pot." I opened the drawer and grabbed the small pot and placed it on the burner, reaching for the bag of quick oats.

"No, you just concentrate on you. I'll get to it a little later. I'll just have my coffee first," she said, using her cane to make her way over to the dinner table where she sat down and took a sip of her coffee.

I flipped my eggs over and then looked at Aunt Vi. She looked tired. Too tired for only having been up for an hour or so. "Are you feeling okay today?" I questioned.

"Oh, I'm just a little achy this morning, Pet. Just the normal. I can certainly tell that fall is on its way."

I nodded. "Are you going to come down and help me open the bookstore this morning?"

Aunt Vi looked at me and shook her head. "No, dear, I think I'm going to stay up here with my heating pad and work on my needlepoint. Besides, I think my days of running that bookstore are over."

I was just about to take my eggs out of the pan

when her words caught me by surprise, and I stopped. I never thought I'd hear those words from Aunt Vi. She'd run this bookstore since she had been in her twenties, perhaps even earlier. "What do you mean?" I asked, a shiver running through me.

"Pet, bring your breakfast over here and come sit down. I want to talk to you about something." She patted the chair in front of where my coffee sat.

I dumped my eggs onto my plate beside my lightly buttered toast and carried the plate over, sitting down, my stomach turning in anticipation of what she wanted to talk to me about. I'd just taken my first bite when Aunt Vi reached into the pocket of her robe and pulled out a brochure and slid it in front of me.

"Retire in comfort," I read aloud. "Willow Valley's new retirement complex has much to offer." I frowned as I turned the brochure over, barely glancing at the rest of the words printed on it. "I don't understand. What is this?"

"Pet, I put my name on the list over a year ago, while they were still building. I never mentioned anything because at the time I wasn't even sure if it was what I wanted, but as time went on, I know I am now ready to retire and pass the store on to you. I don't want to be a burden to you with doctors' trips and looking after me. You have enough to deal with, especially with the store."

"Aunt Vi, don't be silly. You looked after me all these years."

"Ah, but you were easy, dear. You always were a good girl, and you barely got in the way of anything," she said, smiling at me the way she always did. "I fear that I will put too much pressure on you, so I put my name in."

My stomach sank at the fact she thought she would ever be too much trouble for me. She was all I had. I wasn't married, I had no children… Well, except Luna, and now that we'd hired Ava, if I needed to be away from the store for a bit, it didn't matter. I had no idea what it was she was getting at.

"Anyways, they called me about two weeks ago. There is a suite for me there. I'll be with people my own age, and they have games and trips, a pool, plus my suite has a small kitchen so I can either cook my own meals or I can sit in and eat with the others."

"I see that," I said, opening the brochure to take a closer look.

"Trinity, it's time, dear. It's time for you to take over the running of the bookstore. Besides, you should be out dating and bringing men back here. Not living like an old lady like me."

I took a drink of my coffee, still shocked at what I was hearing. "Aunt Vi, there is no need for you to move out, and we aren't going to start on the dating front.

You know how I feel about that. I have no problem taking over the bookstore, no problem at all, but I can still look after you as well."

"Oh, my dear, my joints ache, the stairs are getting harder for me to navigate. I can't even bend to maintain my gardens any longer. This will be good for me. Plus, they have health care right on site. I won't need for anything."

The lump that sat in my throat was growing bigger by the second, and I swallowed hard as the words on the brochure went out of focus. Aunt Vi was the only family I had; she was all I had, and the thought of her leaving made me want to cry.

"I've already given them my move-in date. I'll be moving in on Tuesday."

I looked around our small two-bedroom apartment, wondering what the place was going to look like after she left. Most of the things here were hers, which would mean I would have to furnish the small two-bedroom apartment.

"Don't worry, the only things I'm taking with me are what's in my bedroom. My suite is fully furnished, but I want my own bed and my recliner. They have all the other stuff I need there. So, the apartment won't be empty." She rested her warm hand on my forearm, her way of comforting me.

I looked at Aunt Vi, wondering to myself how it

was that she read my mind. "How did you know I was worried about that?"

"Because I know you," she said, patting my hand. "I could already see you trying to figure out what you would need to order," she said, smiling.

"All right, I will post a notice on the door that we will be closed on Tuesday then, or see if Ava can fill in. I'll take you and make sure I like the place, make sure you like the place, and that you get settled in okay."

"Sounds good, dear. Oh, and look at the time. It's going to be nine before you know it. You better get down there. Customers will be waiting." Aunt Vi smiled at me.

I could barely smile back, but I did it anyway as I picked up my plate and downed the rest of my coffee. I made my way down the stairs from our apartment to the store and flipped on the lights. I went over to the door and flipped the sign and the lock and went about my daily checklist. My heart was heavy at the thought of her leaving, and I'd spent the first few minutes trying not to cry. When I'd completed my opening list, I stopped and looked around the small bookstore. The old wooden shelves were worn and scratched, same with the old wooden counter. The place could use a coat of paint as well, I thought. I'd wanted to fix it up for years, but Aunt Vi loved it the way it was, so I never mentioned anything. Now that she was moving on, I decided that now may be a good time to start. I also wondered about possibly expanding. The lot beside us had sat empty for years, and I knew Aunt Vi and I had talked about it. I grabbed my notepad and pen and jotted down a quick list of the things I'd like to fix. I'd need something to focus on after she'd moved.

It was almost dark when I pulled the car into the small driveway and walked around the back of the house and slid my key into the lock. I climbed the back stairs to the small apartment and stopped at the top. Luna was in the front window, basking in what was left of the sun for the day. I stopped, slipped my shoes off, and dropped my purse on the couch and looked around the apartment. It was oddly quiet, and I reached for the remote and turned on the TV to drown out the silence.

I'd taken Aunt Vi over to the retirement village today and had gotten her settled in. She seemed happy and excited, and I'd spent the day with a forced smile on my face, until I'd returned. I'd never felt so alone on my drive home, but if I thought that was alone, I'd been wrong. This is alone, I thought to myself as I wandered into the kitchen where I pulled a frozen dinner from the freezer, removed the box, and threw it into the microwave that sat on the counter.

I wandered down the hall and stopped just outside Aunt Vi's bedroom. I expected to see her sitting in her chair, working on her needlepoint, but the room now was completely empty. It was so strange to see it empty. I stepped inside and wondered what I would to do with that room. I heard the beeping of the microwave and made my way back to the kitchen, pulling the now hot dinner onto a plate, and carried it into the living room where I sat down on the couch.

I looked around the room as I ate, thinking I could perhaps give myself a little more space in the living room for another chair and make Aunt Vi's old bedroom an office. Yet part of me still hoped she would call any minute and tell me to come and pick her up. I'll hold off, I thought to myself. Nothing had to be done right away.

I dug into my dinner, reached for the remote, and flipped the channel to *The Golden Girls*, smiling to myself. Aunt Vi and I always watched them in the evening during dinner. Soon I'd eaten my dinner and curled up under a blanket, with a hot cup of tea at my side. Luna jumped down from the windowsill and jumped up onto my lap, rubbing her head on my chin, purring loudly. I pulled her into me, and for a moment, I didn't feel completely alone.

CHAPTER 5

Thomas

I drove down the long driveway of what used to be my home. Nothing had changed, well perhaps the sign that hung over the driveway had. The worn wooden sign had begun to show its age, and it looked as if it hadn't been painted in what looked like years. I noticed the fences that edged the driveway were also in need of some repair. As I slowed my truck, I saw a lot of broken areas. When I'd hit the top of the hill and the house came into view, everything about it looked worn.

I'd just cut the engine when the front door opened and out stepped someone I didn't recognize. The stranger on the porch watched my every move as I climbed out of my truck and shut the door.

"Can I help you?" he yelled from the shadows of the porch.

"Thomas Jenkins. Who are you?" I called.

"Thomas? Thomas? Is it really you?" the old man questioned. "It's Lyle."

I took a harder look at the man who was now walking down the stairs of the front porch, cane in hand, as he made his way over to me. As he approached, I saw some familiar features in his face. Sure enough, it was Lyle—much older, but it was Lyle. He approached me, his hand out.

"Lyle, it's good to see you," I said, placing my hand in his, then hugging the man I used to know.

"Sorry about your father, kid."

"Thanks. What happened?" I questioned.

"Heart attack out in the field. We did everything we could, but the doctor said he was gone before he even hit the ground."

I swallowed hard, the thought of never seeing my father again weighing heavy on me for the first time since I'd heard the news. I looked up at the house and then out to the barn and noticed more of the fences were beginning to fall. "Place looks like it's in bad shape." I said, looking up at the house.

"It's not like it used to be, that's for sure. Most of

the ranch hands are gone now. I've been pretty much running the place since your mom passed and your father's health took a turn. It was almost as if once she was gone, your father lost his love for the place. We have three horses and about twenty cattle, that's it. It's a lot for me to look after now, but it gets done."

"Looks like you're in bad shape yourself, Lyle," I said, nodding to the cane.

"Ah just my sciatica bothering me. I'll be fine."

I nodded, looking out over the empty fields that used to be filled. I glanced to my watch. "Listen, I need to head into town. I have to meet with the funeral director, and then I have a meeting with a lawyer."

"Well bring your stuff inside. Your old room is available. I've been staying in the guest room. I hope that is okay."

"Of course, Lyle. I'm not here to kick you out," I said, making my way over to my truck and pulling my bag out from the back seat. "Besides, it will be nice to have some company."

It had taken almost the remainder of the day to finish up with the funeral director and the attorney. It had been a blur of information; all I knew was that I had a lot of decisions to make in a very short time. I stepped out into the street and glanced around at the familiar town. A lot had changed in the years I'd been gone.

I looked around. Some of the businesses I still recognized, many others I didn't. I went over to my truck and climbed in. Starting the engine, I pulled away from the curb. I drove down the road and stopped at a light, glancing to my right. I read the sign above what used to be the old laundromat and pulled over. I needed a flower shop, and Peggy's Petals was probably the only one in town.

The chimes over the door rang out as I entered. A woman stood behind the counter working on an arrangement. "I'll be right with you," she sang, poking her head over the arrangement in front of her.

"Take your time, no rush," I said, removing my hat.

I took a moment and looked around the storefront. Her arrangements were beautiful, I thought to myself, and since I needed to provide flowers to the funeral home, I figured this was the place.

"What can I do for you?" She smiled, wiping her hands on her apron and grabbing a pencil and a pad of paper.

"I need to place an order for flowers."

"I think I can do that for you," she said, glancing

around with a smile and winking. "What's the occasion?"

I shoved my hands in my pockets. "It's for a funeral. My father's funeral," I murmured, swallowing hard. No matter how many times I'd heard it or said it, it still didn't seem real, but the regret I felt for not speaking to him all these years was very real, and it was beginning to eat at me.

"Oh my, I'm so sorry for your loss." She reached under the counter and placed a book down in front of me on the counter. "Here are some samples of the arrangements I've done in the past. I have most of the flowers in stock. Depending on when the arrangements are needed for, I can order different things in as well."

"I don't know much about flowers," I muttered as I flipped open the book and flipped a couple of pages. "I think I'll go with this one, and two of these," I said, pointing to the images on the page.

"Good choice. Those are very popular. When do you need them for?"

"Monday. They need to go to the funeral home over on…"

"Oh, I know where it is, no worries. They will be there."

I watched as she rang up the order and passed me the debit machine. I slid my credit card into the machine and waited for the approval message.

"Is there anything else I can do for you?" she asked.

I cleared my throat, my curiosity getting the best of me. "Do you happen to know if Bluebird Books is still around? It used to be run by Vi…."

The lady, whom I assumed was Peggy, looked back at me and smiled. "Why yes, it is. I believe they are still open too. They close at seven on Friday's, I believe," she said, glancing at her watch. "You've got time."

"Great, thank you." I reached for a small bouquet of carnations from a bin. "I'll take these as well," I said, pulling a twenty from my wallet.

I left the flower shop and hopped into my truck, placing the flowers on the seat beside me. I drove down Bluebird Street, finally seeing the front of Bluebird Books coming into sight. It looked exactly as I remembered, but upon closer inspection, I noticed it, too, needed some repair. Vi, if she still owned it, would be getting up there in age, and my stomach tingled at the thought that Trinity may still be here. I had no idea what had prompted me to drive down here because I figured if Trinity was still here, she would be married by now with a couple of kids, and that was something I didn't need to know. It was like I wanted to torture myself for the choices I'd made.

I pulled up to the curb and watched as a couple of young kids came out of the front door, taking off in the opposite direction. My mind instantly went to thoughts of what our children would have been like had we married. I shook my head and the thought disappeared almost as fast as it had appeared.

What if Trinity was working here? There was no way I could just drop in and face her. I tried to see inside the shop, but I was too far away, so I just sat there staring up at the place. After a few minutes, I decided to just head back to the ranch and put the truck into drive, but something stopped me, and instead of pulling away, I put the truck in park and cut the engine.

I got out of the truck, grabbed the flowers I'd gotten for Vi, and slowly approached the store, glancing in through the window. I couldn't see anyone, so I took a deep breath and opened the door, walking into the small store. In that moment, it was as if I had been transported back through time and I was suddenly eighteen again. The store still smelled the same: books and gardenias. I glanced at the wall on my left and took in some of the titles on the shelves. Then out of the corner of my eye I saw some pictures. I walked over and looked at them. Instantly, I recognized Vi standing out front with a young Trinity and I smiled to myself.

"Be right out," I heard a voice call from the back.

My stomach flipped at the sound of the voice. My

mind had to be playing tricks on me. There was no way that could really be Trinity. I turned to look at the books on the shelf to my right and picked one up, flipping through the pages.

"Sorry about that. What can I help you with?" I heard behind me.

I turned in the direction of a voice I'd recognize anywhere, holding out the flowers as the smile fell from my lips. Trinity stood before me. She was older, looked more tired than I'd ever seen her look, but she was still as beautiful as she was all those years ago. Only this time there was no smile. Instead, a look of shock and surprise was on her face. She stared back at me, lost for words.

We stood there for a moment, looking at one another, neither of us saying anything. My eyes floated from her golden hair to her pale-blue eyes, down the curves of her body and back to her eyes.

"Thomas?" she questioned. "Is it really you?"

"Yeah, Trin, it's me. These are for you. It's been a long time. How are you?"

Instead of taking the flowers from me and answering my question, she turned her back on me and began removing books from the box that sat on the counter in front of her. It wasn't exactly the warm welcome I'd imagined or hoped that I would get. Was it possible she was still angry after all these years?

There was no way she could hold a grudge that long. I placed the flowers down on the worn counter and picked up a book from a box on the table that was in front of me, flipping it in my hand. "So, after all these years, you aren't going to say anything to me?" I questioned, and cleared my throat, placing the book back in the box and grabbing another one with a beautiful leather cover.

"Thomas, I don't know what you want, but I really don't have anything to say to you."

"I came in for a book. I needed something to read," I answered.

"With flowers?"

"Yes."

"Then just pick something." She turned and glared at me, then glanced down to the flowers on the counter.

"Trinity, please…a lot of time has passed. I think-"

She stopped what she was doing and turned toward me, her hands on the counter in front of her. "Yes, a lot of time has passed. Still, I have nothing to say to you, Thomas. If you came in here to buy a book, just take one—any one. There will be no charge. Just take it and go, please." There was a slight tremor in her voice, and as I looked closer at her, I could see her eyes were lined with pain.

I frowned and looked down to the book in my

hand. Trinity hadn't changed. It was just like her to kick someone out, followed with a please. "I guess I will take this one," I said, holding up the leather-bound book in my hand.

"Just take whatever one you want. Take two, three, the whole box, I don't care," she bit out, turning away from me.

I looked after her, then turned and made my way to the door, my head hung low. I turned one more time before I exited. She still stood with her back to me, not moving. I didn't want to press the issue any further than I already had. I left the flowers on the counter and opened the door, allowing it to fall closed behind me, and I went over to my truck and climbed in and started the engine.

I sat out on the front porch of the home I'd known growing up, enjoying the night air and silence. When I'd returned from town, I'd spent some time looking around. The more I looked, the more I realized that the place was not only in bad shape. It was probably far beyond repair, in some cases. I wasn't sure how much it would take to repair, or how much money it would take even if I wanted to at this point. It might just be best to put the place up for sale and pass it on to someone who would love it the way my parents had.

I took a sip of my coffee, thinking of all the things I'd need to do around the house before I had a pile of people here for the wake. I knew Lyle would give me a hand, since he'd already offered. I placed my coffee mug on the small table that sat beside me on the porch and picked up the book I'd gotten from the bookstore. I ran my hand over the leather cover. I hadn't even opened it to see what it was. I'd been so shocked at the fact that Trinity wouldn't take a couple of minutes to talk to me, I just took what was in my hand.

I opened the front cover to a blank page. Two hand-drawn hearts were there, the names *Jed and Vi forever* written underneath. I frowned, then turned the next page. A date was scrawled in pretty handwriting on the next page: July 5, 1966. My curiosity getting the better of me, I flipped the page to see *Dear Diary* written in the same pretty handwriting.

Was this Vi's diary? I questioned. It had to be. I read a little further and then decided that I'd need to return this to Trinity. It must have gotten into the box by mistake. I shut the journal and set it down on the small table, my eyes wandering to the flower beds in front of the house, then back to the diary. Then I reached for the book again, my curiosity getting the better of me. I opened it back up to the first page, but within minutes shut it again. I had no right to read someone's personal thoughts.

I placed it on the table beside me and picked up my coffee cup. I glanced out over the fields. The sun was just beginning to set, providing a beautiful reddish-orange hue over everything. For some reason, I knew it would be hard for me to let this place go, but I knew there was no way I could keep it. I'd never been interested in running a ranch.

The longer I sat there with my own thoughts, the more I wanted to get out of my head. I looked back to the small table where I'd placed the book and let out a deep sigh. "Oh what the hell," I muttered to myself. I picked up the book, opened it up to the center, and began reading.

CHAPTER 6

Trinity

I carried my coffee into the bookstore and placed it down on the counter. It had been a late night, and I'd barely gotten any sleep. I'd spent the night tossing and turning, only to rise early to try and stop the thoughts of Thomas from consuming my mind. I looked up at the little clock that sat above the register; it was almost nine. I walked over to the sign in the window and flipped it over, then opened the front door and wedged a piece of wood underneath it to allow the fresh fall air to pour in.

It was going to be a beautiful day. The sun shone

brightly, and the streets were already bustling with people. I waved to a couple of girls who walked by.

"Morning, Trinity!" they both shouted.

"Morning, girls," I called back, then pulled out the welcome sign and set it out front of the store.

I went back inside and grabbed my clipboard from behind the counter, making my way over to one of the bookshelves, and began taking inventory of what books had sold.

"Good morning!" I heard behind me and turned to see Peggy in the doorway, a box from The Crispy Biscuit tucked securely under her arm.

"Morning," I said unenthusiastically.

"Well, if I had of known you'd be this excited to get your coffee cake muffin, I'd have ordered you two." Peggy giggled, sitting down in one of the chairs that sat in the corner.

"I'm sorry, I had a bad night," I said, placing my clipboard down on the counter and crossing my arms in front of me. "How are you?"

"Good. I can't stay too long this morning. I had a huge order for some funeral arrangements. Plus. I need to get all the baskets done for Mrs. Parker as well."

"Funeral? I've been so busy that I'm behind on all the town gossip. I almost feel as if I live in another universe right now. Who passed away?"

"William Jenkins. His son came in yesterday to

order the flowers for the funeral. Oh, did he stop by? He asked about the store by name, so I'm guessing he used to live here at one point," Peggy said as she peeled the wrapper away from the soft, cakey muffin.

Peggy had only moved to Willow Valley about four years ago, after she lost her husband. Even though we became friends almost instantly, I'd never told her about Thomas. Some things were just better left buried, and Thomas Jenkins was one of them.

I felt my stomach turn. That explained it completely. That was why Thomas was back here. It had to be. There'd be no other reason. I walked over, picked up the muffin Peggy had brought for me, and removed the paper, then I buried my teeth into the sweet cake, savoring every bite.

"Did you want coffee?" I asked with my mouth full.

"Yes, please. I'm going to need the energy." Peggy giggled.

I brought out a fresh, hot cup of coffee and set it on the counter, noticing that Peggy was looking at me, a look of concern on her face. "Trinity, is something wrong? Where's Vi?" she asked, looking down the hall toward the back.

"She moved to the new retirement village. I dropped her off there on Tuesday. She said she was ready to retire. I'm not going to lie. It came as a shock, to be honest."

"Is that what's got you so down?"

"No, if she is ready to retire, I say let her. I'm happy for her. What I'm not happy about is the visitor I had last night," I said, taking a sip of my hot coffee and setting it back down.

"Oh? Is it something I should be worried about?" Peggy asked, taking a sip of her coffee.

"Not unless you have the same ex I do," I said, shoving another piece of muffin into my mouth.

"Ex? You have an ex?" Peggy questioned, looking at me with big, rounded brown eyes.

"Unfortunately, I do. I know most people around here think I'm just some book-loving spinster, but I did date someone a long time ago."

Peggy couldn't help but start to laugh at my choice of words. "What happened?" Peggy sat back in the chair, getting comfortable, waiting for my story.

"The usual, girl meets boy, girl falls for boy, and then boy runs off and joins the western version of the circus."

Peggy couldn't help but laugh again. "Trinity what are you talking about."

I blew out a breath and sat down in the chair across from her. "Thomas Jenkins happened. We were supposed to get married at the end of the summer after we graduated high school. He was going through a real rocky period with his father at the time. I remember it like it was yesterday. We were having breakfast at The Crispy Biscuit, and he ran into a man who used to work for his father. He had left to join the rodeo, and he had invited Thomas to come down to Darling Ranch to check it out. Without me knowing, he went later that day. That night he dropped the bomb that he was leaving Willow Valley."

"Thomas Jenkins? As in William Jenkins' son?"

"That would be him." I nodded.

"So, he left for good? He left his parents behind?"

"Yep, Mr. Jenkins was always busy with the ranch. Betty used to come and have tea with Aunt Vi often after he'd left. She'd always ask about me, but I did my best to keep my distance. I was hurt enough."

"So, you mean after all these years he never came back?"

"Oh, he did, once, maybe twice over the years. I followed his career for a little while after he left, and I know for a fact that he was here for his mother's funeral or at least he had come into town when she died. I never did see him at her funeral, so perhaps he didn't go. I just heard it from some of the others around town. I assume he came into town, had a fight with his father, and left again. After that, I never heard anything about him. He certainly never tried to find me, until now."

"And how did he do in his career?"

I shrugged. "He did well, but I had to stop watching after a while. He was gone, and it was unhealthy to sit and wonder about someone who you knew wasn't coming back. Besides, when he left, along with him he took my heart. I couldn't allow him to take more than that."

Peggy was silent. She just sat there staring at me for a bit, nodding in understanding. "I'm sorry. If I had of known, I would have lied and told him that the store had closed or something. I figured he was here to see Vi, since he only mentioned her."

I shrugged. "It's all right. You wouldn't have known. Anyways when he showed up here last night, it shocked the hell right out of me. I didn't know what to say. He, of course, acted as if everything was normal between the two of us. I just wanted him to leave. I couldn't even look at him without every feeling I ever had for him rushing right back into me. I had to do whatever it took to protect myself, so I told him to just take a book and go."

"What happened?"

"Exactly what I figured would happen. He took the book and left." I shrugged. "He hasn't changed. He's still running."

"Who's still running."

Both Peggy and I jumped at the sound of a man's voice behind us. I turned and looked toward the door to see Thomas standing there, holding the book he must have taken last night in his hand.

I swallowed hard as I looked at the man I'd been in love with my entire life. He leaned up against the door, wearing perfectly fitted jeans, a blue plaid shirt that brought out his eyes. The sleeves of the shirt were rolled up, exposing his muscular forearms, and he held his hat in his large, rough hands. Large, rough hands that I'd kill to have hold me once again. I swallowed hard.

"Oh gosh, look at the time. I must be going. I've got to get to work. I'll see you soon," Peggy said, getting up from the chair, grabbing her purse and coffee.

Thomas stepped to the side to let her pass before turning to look at me. We stood there in silence looking at one another.

"Oh gosh, where is my head. Trinity, I almost took your mug," Peggy said, running back inside, setting the mug down on the counter as she smiled and winked at me. Before I could say anything to her, she was gone again.

Thomas and I stood there for what felt like an eternity, in silence, looking at one another. My heart felt like it was going to beat out of my chest. I blinked and averted my eyes, grabbing my clipboard. I quickly turned to the shelves behind the counter to keep my distance from him.

"I figured I'd bring this back. I believe it may have gotten into the box it was in by mistake."

"Is that so?" I bit out, not looking at him. "Not the type of reading material you were looking for?"

"It appears to be your aunt's diary. I thought perhaps you might like to read it. The little bit I read is rather interesting," he said, placing it on the counter.

I dropped the clipboard down on the counter and spun around. "Why would I want to read it. Wait! What? You read it?" I asked, shocked.

Thomas shrugged, a slight smile coming to his lips. "Oh, not that much really. Just a little bit of it. However, I think you should read it."

I reached for the book, but before I could grab it, Thomas placed his large hand down on it first. "You look exhausted, and it looks like you could use some help around here," he said, looking around the book shop.

"So?"

"So, I thought that while I'm in town here, maybe I could get some things done for you."

I couldn't help but laugh to myself. "Why would you want to help me? Besides, you're not a handy-man." I looked to Thomas, the expression on his face serious as he stood there. When he didn't say anything,

I grabbed the notepad that sat beside the register and began making a list of all the things that needed to be repaired or repainted, all the things that I had no time to do without shutting down the store for a week or two, then I ripped the paper from the notepad and held it out for him to take. I figured he would take one look at the list and run the other way. Instead, he took the paper and looked down at the list, then lifted his head, his eyes meeting mine, a small smile on his lips.

"What? Let me guess, you aren't interested? That's shocking. I won't expect to see you around here anytime soon," I bit out, an anger I hadn't felt in a long time filling my body.

"No, pretty much the opposite. I'll be here. I have an entire list of things to get done," Thomas said, holding up the piece of paper.

"What? You mean you aren't going to leave like you always do?"

Thomas adjusted his stance and met my eyes. "I left once, Trin. People change."

I put the pencil down and nodded. "And one time was all it took." I glared. "One time to learn a very hard lesson."

"Might I remind you that you had an open offer to join me, or have you forgotten that part?" Thomas snapped. "Don't think for one second I am going to take all the blame here."

He shoved the diary across the counter toward me. Without a word, his eyes met mine as he folded the list neatly in half and shoved it in his shirt pocket. Then he turned and made his way over to the door.

"Well, I'm certainly not going to take it," I bit out, expecting him to walk out, but instead he turned back to me and removed his hat.

"Out of curiosity, what lesson was it that you learned exactly?" he questioned.

"Never to fall in love again," I gritted. "And that you were a huge mistake. You know, come to think of it, I can't remember a day that has gone by that I don't wish I could have taken back everything about us."

Thomas's eyes fell to the floor the instant the words left my mouth. When I realized what I'd said, I wanted to take each word back. I meant none of them, and my heart ached seeing the look on his face. He didn't say anything. Instead, he placed his hat back on his head and stepped out the front door, looking both ways. I just wanted to be left alone right now, and for him to leave, but he didn't. Instead, he turned to me once again. "Where is the hardware store? It's been moved."

Carl's hardware had moved from its old location to a newer building almost seven years ago. "Over off Cardinal Street. Why?"

"Well, I can't exactly do all these repairs without the proper tools and paint, now can I. So, I'm going to go and get those. I will see you a little later." The door shut behind him, and I watched as he stopped and turned around, opening the door once again. "Oh, and, Trinity, I know you don't feel that way. I know you don't think I was a mistake, or that we were a mistake. I certainly don't feel that way about you. So do yourself a favor: take my advice and read the diary."

His words hit me, and before I could say anything, the door shut once again, only this time I watched him walk to his truck. I wanted to stop him and tell him to forget about the list, but before I could get to the door, he'd already driven away. On the surface, I had never been so happy to have someone leave my store. Deep inside, my soul was screaming. I'd been so mean.

I walked over to the chair that sat in the corner and sat down, taking a mental inventory of myself. Then I got up and went into the back storage area and pulled out another box of books and started putting them out. I just needed to keep busy so I could try to keep Thomas Jenkins and all the memories that came with him from my mind.

I lay in the darkness of my bedroom, the day still weighing heavily on my mind. I'd done everything I could think of to try and clear it. I'd watched TV, tried reading one of my favorite authors, worked on some needlepoint. Hell, I'd even gotten a head start on reconciling this month's invoices from the store, and yet here I lay with Thomas on my mind. I kept replaying the conversation with Peggy, and then with Thomas. Then the guilt crept in when I realized that I hadn't even taken a minute to offer him my condolences on his father's passing. What kind of a person had I become? This wasn't how Aunt Vi had raised me.

I ran my fingers through my hair and reached up to turn the small bedside lamp on. Luna slept soundly at my feet, curled up in her usual spot, probably dreaming of chasing mice. I reached for the glass of water I'd placed beside my bed and took a sip, my eyes falling to the brown leather-bound book that Thomas had returned.

I lay back down and stared up at the ceiling, my mind wandering back to that book. I looked over at it; it was like it was calling me, then Thomas's words floated into my mind. 'Read the diary.' I let out a deep breath and then reached over and picked it up, opening it up to the middle of the book. I stared down at my aunt's familiar handwriting. It felt so wrong to read her private thoughts, but I was curious as to why Thomas thought it was so important for me to read. Aunt Vi had always been very private about her past. She never married, never dated, and when I would ask her, she just simply told me that she never found anyone she felt she could spend the rest of her life with.

I flipped back to the front and began reading.

July 5, 1962

Jed Hawkins. That's the only name on my lips and mind tonight. Jenny and I went into town to get some ice cream and we ran into Ben, Jenny's boyfriend. Almost makes me think that was the only reason she asked me to go into town. He was with another boy, Jed and he introduced us. I've never seen a boy like Jed before, so handsome. Dark brown hair, blue eyes, muscular build no doubt from working on the farm, and one of the gentlest smiles I'd ever seen. Jenny and I got our ice-cream and then the four of us walked down by the cove, Jenny and Ben running off to be alone just like they always do, which left me alone with Jed. At first it was awkward being alone with him but then he told me all about moving here to help on the Jenkins farm, and then he wanted to know all about me. No one has ever wanted to know about me.

July 8, 1962

Mama asked me to take some chicken soup up to the Jenkins Ranch. Mama said that Mrs. Jenkins had been down with a flu and thought it would help her out. I walked up the main walkway, stopping to pick a handful of wildflowers to hopefully help brighten her day and that was when I saw him. He stood against the fence, a piece of grass hanging from his lips, watching me. The way he looked at me was something I only ever read in books.

I stopped reading and allowed the book to fall forward. My mind was racing in all directions. Was this the same Jed Hawkins who had persuaded Thomas to leave me all those years ago? Had Aunt Vi had a relationship with him when she was young? I knew Thomas's grandparents had owned the ranch prior to William being born. I blew out a breath and flipped ahead a bunch of pages and continued reading. I still felt as if I were invading her privacy.

June 10, 1964

I snuck out of the house; Jed and I went up to the quarry tonight. Papa would be so angry if he caught me, but it was so worth it. Jed and I lay in the back of his truck looking up at the sky, holding hands and then something magical happened. He kissed me under the stars for the first time tonight. Jenny was right, it was magical, and I think, dare I say it, that I'm in love.

September 15, 1964

What a summer it's been. Papa found out about Jed and me. He was pretty angry, but Jenny stood up for me. Thank goodness for older sisters. She simply reminded him that she started seeing Ben at my age and that Jed was always the most perfect gentlemen. At first Papa continued to yell until Mama pulled him aside. I don't know what she said to him but when he returned, he just sent me off to my room.

September 20, 1964

Jed came with Ben and they both asked Papa if they could take us to the town fair. While I sat on pins and needles, waiting for his answer, Papa looked at me, all I could do was smile. I so wanted to go and hoped he would say yes, which Mama finally convinced him to. After the fair Jed walked me back home. When he leaned in to kiss me goodnight, he whispered in my ear that I was his forever.

I quickly skimmed through the remainder of 1964, mostly every entry shared a date night of some sort, then in May of 1965 I stared at the entry.

May 30, 1965

Jed and I were down at the cove again. He said he'd needed to talk to me. We lay under the big weeping willow tree, wrapped up in a blanket staring up at the mess of branches when Jed rolled up onto his arm and looked down into my face. He leaned down and kissed me so softly, when we parted, he softly smiled. In those few seconds I knew exactly where my future lay and then he asked me to marry him. I told him I couldn't until I was done school, so next year. He agreed and of course I said yes!!!!

May 31, 1965

Jed went with Mr. Jenkins on a road trip for a week. They were bringing a couple bulls down to Texas. Jed was excited to leave, to be able to go to the rodeo, it was his dream. He promised to take me one day. I'm going to miss him while he's gone.

I flipped the page, and the next, and the one after that, but there were no more entries—only dates. I put the book down and grabbed my water. I wonder what happened to them, I thought to myself. There was no way I could wait to find out. I picked the book up and flipped toward the end. I just wanted to find out what had happened; I didn't need to read every personal thought Aunt Vi had.

August 25, 1966

Jed and I are planning to get married in six weeks, Papa and

Mama still don't know. I'm so in love with him. Papa still doesn't care for him, he says he is too irresponsible, too immature, and a dreamer but then Papa likes no one that is interested in his daughters, so I shouldn't be surprised. I just wish he would try to get to know him more, I know he would feel differently, but Papa is insistent that he's only going to break my heart.

September 15, 1966

Jed came back to town tonight. We went out for a drive after dinner. We parked along the trees down at the lake and laid in the bed of his truck. He made love to me for the first time tonight, under the stars. I can't wait to tell Jenny. I know she's done it with Ben, she told me the second it happened.

September 30, 1966

Just when I needed him the most - he's gone. I'll never get over him, he and all other men are dead to me.

October 13, 1966

He's gone, it's gone. My heart is broken. I made Jenny swear not to tell Mama or Papa what happened.

I flipped to the next page, nothing but dates leading into 1968 that simply stopped on December 15. I frowned. What the hell. I kicked the covers off me and I jumped out of bed. Luna raised her head, looking at me as if I were crazy. I quickly made my way down the stairs to the store. Careful not to trip on anything, I made my way over to the counter in the dark to the box that Thomas had pulled this book from. There had to be another diary, there just had to be. I sifted through the books frantically, pulling each one out and looking at the interior in the moonlight that came in through the windows, but there was nothing.

I trudged back upstairs and climbed back into bed, knocking the diary off and onto the floor. I reached over and was about to pick it up when I noticed a piece of paper had fallen out of it. I picked up both the paper and the diary and unfolded the neatly folded letter.

November 12, 1973

Dear Vi,

The road is a lonely place. Over the past few years, I've returned to Willow Valley time and time again. I've sought you out. I saw you the other day coming out of the grocers, you're still as beautiful as you were the day I left. Seeing you again this morning, filled my heart with a regret I can't even begin to explain. I'm sorry I left you, but once I asked your father for your hand, it was too hard knowing that your father would never approve of me. Now as I look back on that, I don't even know why I cared, and I realize what it was that I gave up, what I lost in you, in us. If only you could find it in your heart to give me another chance. I'll be here until next week, I'm willing to change my plans. I'm willing to settle down and provide for you, for us, should you be willing to change your mind and take me back. All you need to do is come to me, as I've done all I could to make you hear me.

Love, Jed

I stared down at the handwriting, tears flooding my eyes. Then I picked up the book and shook it, hoping for another letter to fall, but nothing. I let out a breath. She apparently had not gone to him. I folded the letter carefully and shoved it back into the back of the book. I placed the book down on the night table and reached up and shut the light off. I lay on my back, looking up at the ceiling. What had happened between them?

CHAPTER 7

Thomas

I'd driven into town earlier than I'd expected. It was too early to do what business I needed to tend to, so I decided to grab breakfast at The Crispy Biscuit. Lyle had filled me in on much of the town and told me that Brooke now owned the small diner, and that both of her parents had retired and left it to her.

I parked my truck and made my way to the front of the small diner. It looked like it had been expanded to take over what once had been the small newspaper office. It also looked like everything had been updated from the last time I'd seen it, back when my mother died.

I opened the door and stepped inside and looked around, remembering when Brooke used to serve Trinity and me breakfast when we were younger. I'd also remembered the crush Brooke had had on me back then and how it had driven quite a rift between her and Trinity. The diner hadn't changed much on the inside. They'd expanded, added newer tables, and changed the color of the walls, but otherwise, it was exactly how I remembered it. I stepped farther into the bakery, looking for a table, when I heard someone call my name. I turned and looked in the direction of the dessert counter.

"Thomas Jenkins? Is it really you?"

I nodded and smiled at the short blond girl. "Yes, it's me. How are you, Brooke."

She looked just like she had all those years ago, only a little older. She grabbed a menu and came around the counter, making her way over to me. She guided me over to a table in the corner and set the menu down.

"So, you've finally returned to Willow Valley?" she said, placing one hand on her hip and the other on the back of my chair, waiting for my reply. "Is it permanent or temporary?"

I knew she was probably just searching for gossip.

The Crispy Biscuit always was the hub for all town gossip, and I was already sure there was plenty floating around about me as it was. "Not sure just yet," I replied, opening the menu.

"I see. I heard about your father. I am sorry. I sure will miss seeing his face in here," she said, glancing around at the other patrons. "He was one of my regulars." She winked. "Can I get you a coffee?"

"Thank you, and yes, please," I replied as I read over the menu while she went to grab the pot of coffee. A few new items had been added to the menu, but many of the dishes were still the same as they had been back in my younger years.

"Here you go," Brooke said, filling the mug. "What will you have this morning?"

"Eggs, sausage, and toast," I said, closing the menu and taking a sip of the hot coffee.

"Old habits die hard I see." She winked at me while marking my order down on her notepad. "It will be out in a jiff."

I smiled. I used to order the exact same breakfast years ago when I'd bring Trinity here. I guess Brooke remembered that. I watched Brooke as she walked away, and then I picked up my mug and took another sip of coffee. The coffee even tasted the same. Willow Valley had changed in many ways, and in others it remained the same small town I remembered.

I grabbed a newspaper from the empty table beside me and began flipping through it, reading the occasional article while I waited for my breakfast, and that was when I spotted my father's obituary. The words began to blur as I read them over, and I realized how much I wasn't prepared for tomorrow. In fact, I didn't want to go to a viewing at all, never mind to a funeral later this week, but then who ever does. With a heavy sadness moving over me, I closed the paper and watched people pass by the bakery while drinking my coffee.

It didn't take Brooke long before she appeared with a full plate of breakfast and placed it down on the table in front of me. "Here you are, Thomas."

"Thanks," I muttered.

"So, what are you planning on doing with the ranch. There's rumor that it was left to you. Are you going to start running it again?"

I looked down at my breakfast. "I don't know just yet."

"Well, if you are, you'll have competition. Connor Darling is a hard-working man. You remember him, don't you?" Brooke asked.

I nodded. "I'm not here to compete with anyone," I answered. "As a matter of fact, I might just sell the place. It needs much work."

Brooke nodded in understanding. "Have you had a chance to stop over and see Trinity?" she questioned.

There was the question she'd been dying to ask. I don't know why it even surprised me; it was always like Brooke to ask questions about us. I nodded, reaching for the ketchup, knowing that in a matter of hours, I would probably be the talk of Willow Valley, if I wasn't already, and now I'd be dragging Trinity into it as well. "Yep. As a matter of fact, I'm headed over there to do some work around the bookstore for her."

I could see the curiosity in Brooke's eyes. "Is that so? I guess old habits really do die hard," she muttered. "Well, that's wonderful. I better get moving. Enjoy your breakfast, and welcome back to Willow Valley."

I frowned as I watched Brooke make her way back to the counter and whisper something to the other girl who stood beside her. Perhaps I shouldn't have said anything because there it was. The gossip was starting, and Brooke always did have a knack for starting it.

I dug my fork into my breakfast, ignoring the glances from Brooke and the other woman behind the counter. I'd never been so happy to be finished eating, and I went up right away to pay my bill, ordering a coffee and muffin to-go.

I arrived outside of Bluebird Books a little before nine. The lights were still off in the storefront, and upon quick inspection by peeking through the front window, I could see that Trinity had yet to come down. I glanced at the sign that showed her hours. It told me that she would be open by nine. I placed my hot coffee on the window ledge and went over and removed the ladder from the bed of the truck. I leaned it up against the front of the building and went back over and pulled the large tin of blue paint and the paintbrush I'd purchased yesterday from the back seat of the truck. Then I reached for the sandpaper.

I climbed up the ladder and began sanding away all the flaking paint off the first few letters of the sign, before needing to move the ladder to continue. Once I was finished, I climbed down and cracked the lid of the paint, pouring a little into a plastic container that was easier to hold and climbed back up the ladder and began carefully painting over the words Bluebird Books in brilliant blue. I had only completed the first letter when I heard the front door open, and I looked down to see Trinity.

"What on earth are you doing?" she questioned, irritation lining her voice as she stood looking up at me, her hands on her hips and a frown on her face.

"Uh, well, I believe this was the first item on the list that you wrote down for me," I said, placing the paintbrush down on the top rung of the ladder and pulling the list from my shirt pocket. "Yep, repaint the sign," I said, shoving the list back into my pocket and picking up the brush, carefully dipping it back into the paint.

I looked back down at Trinity and saw her staring back up at me, her arms crossed over her chest and a scowl on her face.

"It never occurred to me to ask, but did you want me to start elsewhere?" I questioned, waiting before moving onto the next letter. "I could fix up the trim around the windows, or you did mention that the gardens needed to be cut back. Of course, there was the shelves. Did you need those done first?"

Trinity stood there not saying anything. Instead, she let out a frustrated sigh and went back into the store shaking her head. I couldn't help but laugh at her irritation, and I went back to painting. By two o'clock, I had finished the main sign over the front of the store and the small sign that stood at the beginning of the path to the back of the house. I gathered up my paint, brushes, and my ladder and threw them into the back of the truck. Then I made my way to the door of the store.

I looked in the front window to see Trinity talking with the lady from the flower shop. I pulled the door open and yelled inside, both of them turning and looking in my direction. I could see the irritation in her eyes as she looked at me. "See you tomorrow." I called, and without giving her a chance to respond I shut the door and made my way over to the truck, climbing into the driver's seat, and pulled away.

I was surprised to see the turnout at the funeral home. I stood at the front of the room speaking with Lyle while I looked around at the people who had gathered. I recognized most of the people here; some I hadn't seen since before I left. I nodded to a couple my parents had known and nodded, then my eyes landed on Trinity. The navy dress she wore hugged her in all the right spots. It was almost hard for me to take my eyes off her.

I'd only seen her when she'd arrived. I'd been so surprised to see her I'd barely noticed what she was wearing. She'd come right over to me and paid her respects, and as quickly as she'd approached me, she'd turned away and made her way over to the far corner of the room to speak with a woman I hadn't seen before. Of course, I'd been busy with everyone arriving, but now that most people had paid their respects and they had formed into small groups talking amongst one another I had more time to notice her.

I couldn't help but keep watching her as she made

her way through the crowd of people, stopping and speaking with just about everyone. She'd always been popular, and with owning the bookstore, there more than likely wasn't a person who lived in Willow Valley that she didn't know.

"So, what are you going to do with the ranch?" Lyle questioned, pulling my attention away from Trinity.

I shrugged. I still hadn't any idea as to what I was going to do with it. I just knew my options were very limited. I could sell it or I could keep it. "I don't know." I shrugged. "I'm not even sure I am going to stay in Willow Valley, to be honest."

"What's that? Did I hear you say that you're not going to stay in Willow Valley? What the hell is wrong with Willow Valley?" I heard behind me.

I turned around in time to meet a pair of eyes I hadn't seen in years.

Jed Hawkins stood before me, crumpled over his cane with a young man who was practically the spitting image of a young Jed beside him.

I blinked hard. "Jed? Is it really you?"

"Yeah, it's me," he said, putting his cane forward and taking a couple steps, the man who I was sure had to be his son making sure he was steady. "For God's sakes, I'm fine. Let go of me." A much older Jed waved his hand at young man.

"Dad, stop being so grumpy. I'm just making sure you are okay."

"Who do you think looked after me all these years before you were born. I'm fine. Now go get me a coffee or something," he snapped.

I looked to his son and couldn't help but smile. Jed had always been a strong individual, and it didn't seem that age had slowed him down any.

"Sorry to hear about your father.," Jed said, coming closer to me. "Heard it was a heart attack."

"Thanks. Yes, so I've been told."

"Did you get to spend much time with him?" Jed questioned.

I shook my head. "No, I moved and followed your advice, never looked back. Over the years we had many fallouts. The last time I saw him was when my mother passed. He wasn't the easiest man to get along with, in case you forgot," I said in a low voice, remembering how cold he had been when I'd returned to say my good-byes to my mother.

I watched as Jed took a step forward, his shaky hand gripping the cane. "You shouldn't have listed to me. That was bad advice I gave you."

I softly smiled. I'd never imagined hearing Jed say those words, yet here I stood. "Well, that advice gave me a life full of adventure. One I probably wouldn't have had otherwise."

"It was still bad advice," he bit out.

"Is that your son?" I questioned.

"Yep. He's a police office here in Willow Valley. Didn't follow in the old man's footsteps." He chuckled. "He was more of a mama's boy. I met her during my last years on the road, shortly before I got injured. We moved back here to raise Jack."

I watched as Jed rocked back and forth, looking uneasy. "Did you want to sit down?" I asked.

"I'm fine," Jed bit out. "You sound just like Jack. He thinks because I'm older I can't do anything for myself. Need I remind you both that I could still handle a full-grown bull."

I couldn't help but laugh. "I don't think that's how he sees it at all," I said, patting Jed on the back.

"Do me a favor and help me get over to that guest-book. I'd like to sign it," Jed said, pointing over to the book that lay on the table.

"Sure thing." I chuckled.

I looked over to where Jack stood speaking with another member of the town and took a step forward, waiting for Jed, only as he took a step forward, he lost his balance, and before I could move fast enough, down he went.

"Jed," I cried, kneeling beside him on the floor. "Are you all right. Are you hurt anywhere?"

"I'm fine," he said, breathing hard. "I just had the

wind knocked out of me." He put his hand beside him and went to move and hissed in pain.

"Jed, perhaps you should just sit there for a few minutes," I said, trying to grab his hand and check him over. "Catch your breath."

Just as I caught his hand Jack came running over. "What happened? Dad, are you all right?"

Jed looked over toward his son. "Nothing happened, I fell. I've fallen plenty of times in my life, just as you have. It's nothing to worry about."

I looked to Jack and saw the concern in his face, and I leaned into him. "I think we should call an ambulance," I whispered. "He tried to put pressure on his hand and get up, but there is pain somewhere. Could be the hip for all we know."

Jack looked to me and nodded, pulling his phone from his back pocket and dialing a number for the ambulance.

"Who are you calling? Get off that phone right now," Jed demanded.

"He's calling the ambulance, Jed. We want to make sure you're fine," I whispered, while Jack spoke to the attendant on the other end of the phone.

"I told you I'm fine," he said and went to try to push himself up again, this time hissing out in pain and pulling his hand up, rubbing his wrist.

"Jed, I don't think you are. Now just relax, don't move. We don't know if anything is broken."

I could tell Jed was irritated with us both as we waited for the ambulance. Thankfully, it didn't take them long to arrive, and we watched as they loaded Jed onto a stretcher and placed him into the back of an ambulance.

I turned toward Jack. "Let me know how he makes out," I said, shaking his hand.

"Sure will. I fear it might be time Dad moves into that new retirement home they just built here. He's getting harder to look after by the day. He's so unsteady on his feet, and I fear leaving him alone when I head to work." He shrugged, looking at me with worry. "Besides, he keeps telling me that is where he wants to go."

"Wait and see how he makes out. If you need help talking to him, I'll come by and have a chat with him. I speak his language, remember."

"I'm glad someone does. I wish Mom were still here. She was always able to get him to do anything. Sadly, she passed on a few years ago."

"I'm sorry to hear that. Please keep me posted," I said, patting Jack on the back. I watched as he made his way to his car and pulled out of the parking spot, following behind the ambulance.

It was nine when I left the funeral home and made my way back to the ranch. I drove up the dark driveway and parked my truck in front of the house. As I climbed the steps, I was surprised to find a few casserole dishes of food on the front porch, each of them containing a small note telling me what the dish was and who it was from. I carried them into the kitchen, carefully putting everything into the fridge. Then I chose one and placed a couple scoops in a bowl and heated it up in the microwave. I sat down in the living room and turned on the small TV. I flipped until I came across a bull riding match and took a bite of the chicken and broccoli casserole.

CHAPTER 8

Trinity

I stood on a ladder, wiping off the tops of the shelves. It seemed they hadn't been dusted in years and looking at them up close, I noticed they could really use a coat of stain. They were in worse shape than I'd thought. I grabbed my spray bottle and sprayed the cleaner over the surface again and taking my cloth, I wiped them clean again.

It had been a slow afternoon, which I was glad about as it gave me time to get some of this cleaning done. Plus, it was nice to be surrounded by the quiet.

Luna lay in the over-sized armchair, sound asleep, curled up on the blanket I'd thrown there.

"There we go, Luna, that shelf is all clean now," I said, carefully climbing down the ladder to grab the stack of books I'd removed and replaced them. It was the last set of shelves I had planned on doing today, so I folded the ladder back up and placed it back in its spot between the bookshelves.

The viewing for William Jenkins had been yesterday. I'd decided to go as it was my day off, but for the funeral, I would have to close the shop in the morning since Ava, the girl who normally helped me in the late afternoon and on weekends, was not available to work. Many members of the town had shown up and shared some memories with each other. I had gone for a few minutes, offered my condolences to Thomas quickly, and then went off to talk with others, leaving shortly thereafter.

Of course, I'd heard that there had been an incident at the viewing. Apparently, Jed Hawkins had come in with his son, Jack, and had taken a nasty fall. I'd heard from Brooke that they had to take him by ambulance to the hospital. I was glad I'd missed him. After all, he was the man responsible for taking Thomas away from me all those years ago.

I ran my feather duster over the books in the romance section and turned abruptly when the bells above the door jingled. Peggy entered the store, a smile on her face as she closed her umbrella.

"Hey!!" she sang, "It's really coming down out there." She shook her closed umbrella just outside the door. It had been raining almost the entire afternoon.

"Yes, that it is," I said, moving toward the window to look outside at the dark-grey skies, just as a crack of thunder rang out. "What's with the clipboard?" I questioned, looking to Peggy.

"Oh, well, I was just making my rounds. Some of the ladies thought it would be nice to take Thomas some food. We got talking after the funeral. You know, to help take the burden off and such."

"That's nice."

Peggy frowned. "So, I just thought I would come by and see what you'd like to contribute."

I let out a loud sigh and went back to dusting the tops of the books. "I have no idea."

Peggy was silent, and I could feel her staring at me from behind. "What's wrong?" she questioned, placing the wet umbrella down just inside the door.

I let out a sigh. I was normally the one who put together these types of things for the members of the community. I was the one running place to place with the clipboard, only this time it hadn't even occurred to me to do anything because I was still dealing with my own issues regarding Thomas and trying to swallow the anger, I felt toward him.

"What do you mean what is wrong? Nothing is wrong!" I exclaimed, placing the duster on the counter and looking at Peggy. "I'm just not impressed with how I've let this place go," I muttered.

"Trinity, you can't fool me. I've known you far too long." Peggy took her light jacket off and placed it on the coat rack, then pulled up one of her favorite stools and sat down, laying the clipboard she'd been carrying on the counter. "You haven't let this place go. So, just spill it."

I walked over and stared down at the list of names on the clipboard and reached for it, pulling it closer to me. Peggy was bringing a chocolate cake, Brooke was bringing mushroom quiche, Melinda was bringing chicken soup, and the list went on. Practically half the town had committed to bringing some sort of dish, and I knew it would look bad if I didn't sign up to bring something.

"Put my name down. I have no idea what I'll bring though."

Peggy picked up the pencil I kept near the register and scribbled my name down on the list. "Now tell me what has gotten to you, my dear."

I poured us both a hot coffee from the pot I'd just brewed a little while ago and sat down. "Were you still at the funeral home last night when Jed Hawkins fell?"

"Oh, I heard about it, but no, I was already gone. I hope he is okay."

I let out a sigh. "He's the reason that Thomas left Willow Valley."

"You mean, he was the one who told him to join the rodeo?"

I nodded, got up and walked around behind the counter. I pulled Aunt Vi's journal from the shelf I'd placed it on and pulled it closer to me. I was still searching for the second half of it. I knew there had to be more, but I still hadn't been able to find it. I also hadn't been able to find any more letters, despite having gone through every box in the back that was marked with her name.

"I guess you could say that this is what has gotten my back up," I said, opening the book and flipping through the pages.

"What is that?" Peggy said, leaning over to try and take a closer look.

"This was the book that Thomas borrowed the other day when he came here for the first time. He brought it back practically the next afternoon, thought I should have it. Actually, he thought I should read it. It's Aunt Vi's journal."

"Oh, I wonder if she is missing it. You should take

it to her," Peggy said, dumping a packet of sugar into her coffee and stirring it. "Wait, what did you say?"

I stared down at the journal. I hadn't read it all, but what I had read I regretted. It was her personal thoughts, after all, and it felt like a total invasion of her privacy. "Thomas thought I should read it, so I read it," I whispered. "Well, not all of it, just some of it."

Peggy stopped stirring her coffee and met my eyes. "You what?"

"That's what has me in such a state. I read her journal, and by the looks of things, Jed Hawkins was the man that she was in love with. He is also the reason why she never married. At least that is what I understood."

"The same Jed Hawkins from the funeral home."

I nodded. "I think so. I mean, I won't know for sure until I ask Aunt Vi, but it certainly appears to be that way," I said flipping through the pages of her journal for what had to be the fiftieth time. "I've never heard of another Jed Hawkins in this area."

"Wow, Trinity, I don't know what to say. Didn't Vi ever tell you anything about her past?"

"No, she has always been very tight-lipped about it. We never really talked about it, to be honest. From what I can see, he broke Aunt Vi's heart. I don't know if I even want to bring it up to her. I have no idea how she will react. Judging from the last few pages of this diary, it looks like it took her a long while to get over him. At least, that is what I'm guessing."

"It's been a long time, Trinity. I am sure the hurt wore off by now."

"Yeah, I sure hope so," I muttered, running my fingers over the leather cover. "Anyways, what to bring?" I said, drumming my fingers on the counter and looking off into the distance.

"You know what you need?"

"What's that?"

"Aunt Vi's chicken and dumplings. That will put all your worries to ease."

I smiled. Aunt Vi always said they were the cure for everything.

"That dish gives me nothing but heartburn." We both giggled at the same time.

"Wait! That is what you could bring for Thomas."

I laughed. I'd remembered the last time Thomas had those; he hated them with a passion. "Thomas hates those. He used to tell me that they were like eating paste."

"So, he's had your dumplings before?"

I giggled. I could tell from the look in Peggy's eyes that she wasn't referring to those dumplings, and I felt my cheeks get hot. I did my best to ignore it and nodded. "Yes, and he really does hate them. So, I guess you're right, that is what I'll bring."

Peggy had stayed until I closed the store, and once she was gone, I got in the car and drove to the small grocery store. I carried the two large bags upstairs and dropped them onto the counter. I began pulling the ingredients for Aunt Vi's famous chicken and dumplings from the bag. Once everything was out on the counter, I pulled my small cookbook from the cupboard and turned to family recipes, then I grabbed the remote and turned the TV on to *The Golden Girls* and began chopping up all the ingredients.

I dredged the chicken in the flour, lighting coating it before placing each piece into the stockpot that sat on the stove top, each one sizzling away. Once I'd placed the last piece into the pot, I began turning each one of them, gently browning the other side. As soon as they were finished browning, I removed them from the pan and went back to chopping up my vegetables.

I dumped the onions, carrots, and celery into the stockpot and let them cook while I chopped some fresh garlic and added that to the mixture. Then I mixed the flour into the vegetables and slowly added the chicken stock, stirring constantly until everything was blended and had begun to thicken. I added in the wine and sugar, bay leaves and peppercorns, and returned the chicken to the pan, bringing it up to a boil, then turning the burner down to a simmer and placed the lid on the pot.

It had been so long since I'd made Aunt Vi's chicken and dumplings that I'd forgotten how good they smelled. Even though this dish gave me heartburn, my stomach growled out loud, and it was just in that moment that I realized I hadn't stopped to eat anything all day. I pulled two pieces of bread from the bag that sat on the counter and made myself a quick peanut butter and jelly sandwich. As I stood there watching *The Golden Girls*, slowly eating my sandwich, I felt Luna rub up against my legs.

"Hey, Luna, are you hungry too?" I questioned, looking toward her empty bowl.

She let out a loud meow as if answering my question. I smiled, rubbed her head and grabbed the can of cat food from the fridge, dumping the remainder into her bowl.

While the chicken was cooking, I quickly stirred up the dumplings and placed them on a baking sheet, then I removed the chicken from the stockpot, skimmed all the fat from the top of the pot, and began pulling all the chicken from the bones, using two forks to shred the meat. Once it was all shredded, I returned that to the pot and turned the burner up, allowing the mixture to boil, then just as I was taught, I placed each dumpling on top of the simmering soup, reduced the heat, and cooked the mixture for another twenty minutes.

I took my time cleaning up the kitchen and made my way down to the bedroom to change my clothes, then went back to the kitchen to check the dumplings, which I was happy to find were perfectly cooked. I shut the heat off and gently stirred in the cream and added some parsley and thyme.

I reached up into the cupboard to find one of my favorite casserole dishes and filled it, keeping half the pot aside for myself, which I left on the counter to cool. I'd place a bowl in the fridge for dinner tomorrow and put one bowl aside for Aunt Vi. I grabbed my purse and keys and carefully carried the hot casserole dish downstairs. As I approached the back door, I saw Aunt Vi's diary sitting on the bench where I'd left it. I wondered if Thomas had read as much of it as I had. I wondered if he knew that Aunt Vi and Jed were once an item. I placed the casserole dish down on the bench and picked up the diary, shoving it into my bag, and then I picked up the casserole and opened the door, locking it behind me.

It was beginning to get dark as I drove up the driveway of the Jenkins farm. I swallowed hard as my nerves kicked in. Why had I agreed to bring this dish up to Thomas? I swallowed hard and looked down at my shaking hands that held the wheel.

"My goodness, you're being ridiculous. Just drop the dish on the front porch like everyone else does and drive away," I said out loud to know one but myself, then laughed at my silliness.

As I pulled up in front of the house, I cut the engine. The ranch hadn't changed; it just needed a little love, I thought to myself. I climbed out of the car, reached into the back seat, and grabbed the hot casserole dish. I slowly walked up to the house and was about to climb the steps to place the dish down on the small side table that sat beside the wicker rocking chair when the porch light came on, my stomach instantly turning.

CHAPTER 9

Thomas

I hadn't been back in Willow Valley for even a week, yet it felt like an eternity. I was sitting in the living room reading the *Willow Valley Gazette* when I heard a car come up the drive. People had been dropping food off on a consistent basis for the last couple of days, and it was getting to the point that I had no room left to put it in my fridge. I'd already started freezing some after all, it was only Lyle and me. I put the paper down, got up from the chair, and looked out the window to see a familiar car drive up to the house. What was Trinity doing here?

I watched from the window as she climbed out of the car and opened the back door, removing a dish from the back seat. I smiled to myself as she looked up at the house, a look of unease on her face. She began walking toward the porch, so I quickly darted to the door and turned the porch light on. While I appreciated the kindness from everyone, I also had done my best to avoid them, allowing them to drop the dish down on the porch and go, but Trinity was different.

First, I never expected her to come out here, but I was glad that she stood on the other side of the front door. Even after all these years being away from Willow Valley, the second I'd laid my eyes on her, I knew in my heart that I'd made a huge mistake in leaving. Even though she looked at me with all the hatred in the world, I could see right through it. She still loved me; it would just take me time to crack through that rough exterior she claimed to have. It was no different when she was younger and I tried to pursue her. First, I had to break through her exterior shell, but once I had done that, she had been mine.

As I flipped the light on, I looked through the window of the door and could see the look of panic that lined her face. I softly smiled, remembering the first time I'd seen that look. It was the first night I'd kissed her. She had given me a million and one excuses as to why we were such a bad idea, but instead of listening to her, I'd grabbed her arms and pulled her in for a kiss. She practically melted right on the spot. Then, as I pulled away, I saw the look. Only this time the look wasn't from kissing her. I pulled the door open and stepped out onto the porch and out into the fresh night air.

"Well, I certainly wasn't expecting you," I said, my tone low.

Trinity stood there, not saying anything. She looked up at me, then looked down to the casserole dish she held in her hands as if she'd forgotten what it was and why she was holding it.

"What's that?" I questioned, trying to glance at what was inside.

"Oh, um, I just thought.... well...I brought you this." She slowly rasied the dish and held it out for me to take.

I rubbed my hands together. "I sure hope it's your chicken and broccoli casserole. It's my favorite." I reached out to take the casserole dish from her and lifted the lid. "I had one the other night from some lady my mom knew, but it didn't hold a candle to the one you make."

"Nope, not my chicken and broccoli casserole. It's Aunt Vi's chicken and dumplings." She smiled.

Instantly, I felt my stomach turn as I got a whiff of the contents. My mind went to the last time I'd had it, remembering the upset stomach I'd had for days afterward. It had never been my favorite dish, even the one my mother made, and as far as I remembered, Trinity knew it.

"Did you want to come in? It would be nice to have company while I eat," I said, swallowing hard at the thought of eating chunky, paste-like balls of mushy flour.

I almost smiled when I took a look at the scared look on her face; it was almost as if I'd asked her to do something against the law. I leaned up against the post and waited for her answer, not saying anything. I planned to do whatever it took to keep her there, so if that meant chowing down on soggy flour, then I'd do it. I wanted us to get past whatever anger, hate, and bad memories we needed to, so we could hopefully get back to normal.

"Oh, you haven't eaten yet?" she questioned, glancing at her watch.

"No, I wasn't hungry earlier, but suddenly I'm starving, and this…well…this looks delicious," I said, almost choking on my own words. "Besides, the house it was too quiet to eat. So how about it, Trinity? Will you join me?"

"Oh, where is Lyle?" she asked, looking around.

"He went into town. Said he was going to have a

couple drinks with one of the hands from Darling Ranch."

I watched as she looked back to her car. I could only imagine what was going through her mind. Was she wondering if she could run back to it and leave without me noticing?

"I'll…I've just got to grab my purse," she said, turning back toward her car.

"Trinity, I don't think you need to worry about your purse way out here," I said, climbing the stairs and holding the front door open for her. "There's no one around for a few miles at least."

I saw a slight smile on her lips, and she nodded. "Oh of course. Silly me." She swallowed hard.

"Come on in," I said, still holding the door for her.

She stood there for a second and then climbed the three stairs and walked past me into the house, stepping out of the way so I, too, could get inside. She stood just inside the door, glancing around, and was about to follow me to the kitchen when she suddenly stopped and bent down to untie her shoes.

"Don't worry about your shoes. Just come on into the kitchen," I said, leading the way and pulling out a chair for her to sit on. I placed the still-warm casserole dish down on the counter and grabbed a plate and glass from the cupboard. "Want anything to eat or drink?" I asked.

"Oh, no, thank you. I already ate."

"You're sure?" I questioned as I dished some of the chicken and dumplings onto the plate, the look of them already making me nauseous. "These look delicious."

"Yes, I am good, thanks."

"Okay, if you say so," I said, taking a glance at her as I poured myself a glass of milk and carried both the plate and glass over to the table. I sat down and reached for the salt and pepper, shaking the contents of both shakers over my plate.

"You'll have to let me know how they are," Trinity said, watching my every move. "It's been a hot minute since I made them." She smiled as she watched me sink my fork into the mess on my plate.

I looked at the gooey contents that hung off my fork and took a breath, then brought the full fork up to my mouth. *Why did it have to be chicken and dumplings? Of all the things she could have made, this was what she brought.* I took the fork and placed it in my mouth, my gag reflex working almost instantly. Just before I swallowed, I picked up the glass of milk and drank some back; it was the only way to get the food down.

"It's great," I lied, my mouth still partially full.

"Oh good. That means I followed Aunt Vi's recipe perfectly." She smiled. "I was worried they wouldn't turn out."

I smiled back, sinking my fork into the soggy mess on my plate and bringing another forkful up to my mouth. "How is Vi?" I questioned, doing whatever I could to avoid placing this food in my mouth.

"Good. She's doing well. I just moved her to the retirement facility that was just built on the outskirts of Willow Valley."

I could feel the sweat begin to trickle down my forehead and wiped my brow with the sleeve of my shirt before taking another bite, followed by a mouthful of milk. I couldn't help but wonder how much more torture I was going to have to endure, how much more of this I was going to have to eat.

"Are you sure you don't want any?" I asked, nodding to my plate. "Feels a little odd to be the only one eating."

"No, I'm good. I was munching on chicken and vegetables while I made it."

It was the moment that I caught sight of her lip twitching as her eyes danced at my question. *Was she actually enjoying watching me suffer as I ate this mess?* I wondered as I wiped my brow again, this time with my napkin.

Shoving another forkful into my mouth, my stomach churned. There was so much flour, and I seriously didn't know how much more I would be able to eat. I had barely put a dent into what sat on my plate, and my stomach was already turning. With my hand shaking, I wiped my brow again and then brought another mouthful up to my lips.

"All right! That's enough." Trinity said, standing up.

"What?" I asked, shocked at her outburst.

"Do you want to die?" she said, ripping the fork from my hand and dropping it down onto my plate. "You'll end up with heartburn for days on end, you silly man."

I dropped my fork down on the plate and grabbed my milk and drank it down, chuckling as I wiped my face with a napkin. "Well, without you, Trin, I have no reason to live."

"Oh please," she said as she pulled the plate away from me and took it over to the sink. She opened the cupboard where my mother kept the garbage pail and dumped the contents into the bag. "If that were truly the case, you never would have left me in the first place."

I chugged down some milk and stood up, moving toward Trinity. "You know I was just a stupid kid when that happened. Cut me a little slack, would you?" I placed my hands on either side of her body as I leaned against the counter, blocking her in.

"Slack?" she said, turning abruptly so she could look me directly in the eyes. I could feel the heat from her body, could smell the scent of her perfume and my body responded accordingly. "Take all the slack you want, Thomas. It's time for me to go." She slipped right out from under me and headed out the front door.

I ran after her and out the front door. "Trinity, come on, let's talk about this," I called, quickly catching up to her. I was just about to her when she stopped and turned toward me.

"There isn't anything to talk about," she bit out.

"Isn't there? I beg to differ. I can tell that something has been weighing on your mind since I walked into the bookstore. You and I both know you'll feel better if you get it off your chest. Say what you want to say and get it over with. Let's just clear the air between us and move on."

Trinity looked at me, then looked away, letting out a breath. She wanted to say something, I knew she did, and I would eventually get it out of her. I stood there, my hands on my hips, waiting.

"Okay, fine, I have one question."

"All right, and I might have an answer for you," I said, waiting.

"Did you ever hear anything about Jed ever dating anyone when he was younger?" she questioned.

I frowned. "Jed? As in Jed Hawkins?" I asked, standing there completely confused.

Trinity nodded her head, looking at me with curiosity.

Where was that coming from, I wondered. I was sure Jed had dated many women; however, with him being so much older than I was, he certainly wouldn't have confided in me. I shook my head. "Not to my knowledge. I know he was married sometime later in life, but never heard anything about him dating. Why?"

Trinity didn't answer me. Instead, she walked over to the car and opened the driver's door. She bent down and reached into the car and dug around in frantic search of something.

"Trinity, come on," I called, feeling more and more frustrated. "Can you please tell me what this is about?" I'd wanted to talk about us, to clear the air about us, not talk about Jed Hawkins.

"This is why." She stood up, a couple of strands of hair falling into her face. She walked around the car and shoved a familiar looking book in my direction.

"What's this?" I asked, taking the book from her and flipping it over in my hand.

"That is the book you returned to me. Aunt Vi's journal. I read it."

I looked at Trinity. She wore an uncomfortable expression on her face. "Okay. So, like I told you, I glanced at a few parts myself."

"Well, I think she and Jed dated," she whispered to

me as if someone else were going to hear.

"So, what if they did," I whispered back.

Trinity looked at me and shook her head as if I should have understood what she was trying to tell me. Instead, she just looked at me, climbed in her car, and started the engine. I was about to hand the book back to her, but she shook her head. "Just read it. All of it, because you clearly only read a little bit of it!" she yelled and backed the car up. "Let me know what your thoughts are."

I watched as her car drove down the driveway, kicking up dust as it went. She was right. I'd only read a couple of passages, and once I'd seen that Vi had been hurt as well, I'd hoped to show Trinity that she hadn't been the only one. I'd had no idea who the man was or even what had happened between the two of them. It hadn't felt right to snoop.

As soon as her car was completely out of sight, I flipped the book back over in my hands. I climbed the stairs and went back inside the house. I poured a cup of coffee and slipped two sugars in and then made my way back out to the front porch. Taking a sip of the coffee, I looked out over the empty fields. I still had no idea what I was going to do with the ranch, but I had time to figure it out. I blew out a deep breath, took another sip of coffee, and opened the book, starting at page one.

CHAPTER 10

Trinity

I'd woken up with a bit of a headache, just as I'd done the day before. The only difference was this morning the headache seemed to be getting worse. I'd taken my time getting ready, having a hot shower to try and ease the tension I felt in my neck, but it did little good. I'd had some lightly buttered toast for breakfast and then made my way downstairs to open the store.

I flipped over the open sign and unlocked the front door and stepped out onto the sidewalk. The streets of Willow Valley were quiet this Wednesday morning, despite it being a beautiful sunny fall day. I went back inside and returned with the watering can and carefully watered the window boxes full of blue petunias. Every single year, Aunt Vi had planted these, and even though she had retired, I doubted I would ever plant anything else. There wasn't much more life left in them for this year, but I still carefully removed all the dead flowers just as Aunt Vi had shown me. I planned to try and make them last as long as they could. Once I was finished, I backed up and looked up at the newly painted sign.

Thomas had done a fantastic job. The old paint had been peeling for a few years and the words had looked dull, but now it was vibrant, and the old sign looked brand new. Then I looked to the windows. At some point, he had even sanded and started painting the window frames a bright white.

"Morning, Trinity." I turned to see Janice, my neighbor, heading down the street on her way to work.

"Morning. It's a beautiful day isn't it!" I called.

"It is! Oh, I wanted to tell you I just love the new sign. Looks fantastic. Have a great day, Trinity. I will stop by this weekend to get a new read." She waved as she hurried off down the road.

I smiled to myself and then made my way inside. I poured a cup of coffee and carried my mug over to the counter, sitting down on the stool and rubbing my temples. Ever since I'd gotten home the other night, I'd felt this tension headache, and since I hadn't seen Thomas yesterday, I worried that he might never show his face around here again, especially after the dumplings.

I grabbed my sales binder from under the counter and started going over my ledger when the two little bells that hung over the door jingled. I looked up to see Peggy come walking in.

"Good morning! That sign looks amazing. I may have to hire Thomas to help me out over at the flower shop," she said, carrying a familiar pink box under her arm. "Breakfast is here," she sang.

I got up and poured her a hot cup of coffee and then made my way over to the counter, removing a blueberry muffin from the box and taking a bite, even though I wasn't hungry.

"It does, doesn't it." I softly smiled.

Peggy nodded, taking a sip. "So, how did the chicken and dumplings go over?"

I let out a sigh. "Well, dammit, he ate a lot of the dish, even though he hates it."

Peggy looked at me, not sure whether she should laugh or not. "What do you mean? You seriously took him a dish he didn't like? I totally thought you were kidding about that."

"No, I was completely serious. But yes, he sat there

eating down the bowl of chicken and dumplings, sweating and looking like he was going to be sick in order to keep me there."

Peggy laughed. "I can't believe you did that. If you knew he didn't like them then why did you make them?"

I let out a breath. "You know I asked myself the same question when I got home that night. I don't think I have an answer for you. My only reason that I can figure is that I found it so odd that he sought me out and that he has been wanting to spend time here that perhaps I'd see if I could drive him away. The only other reason I have is that I had to do it."

Peggy shook her head. "What? What do you mean you had to do it?" Peggy questioned, looking in my direction.

"Well, I wanted to see if he was serious about being around me. It sounds ridiculous, I know, but the fact that he ate almost the entire plate of something he hates just so he could spend time with me told me all I needed to know."

I could tell Peggy didn't know what to say, and sure it was immature of me to do what I'd done, but at least I knew where I stood.

"Wow, Trinity…that's really messed up."

I smiled. "I know, but I've missed him, Peggy. I just

hadn't realized how much until he stood here the other day, and even though there wasn't a lot of words passed between us, the feelings I'd felt then are still there now."

"You've missed him, yet you made him eat something he hates, and you've treated him like garbage since he appeared." She shook her head with a smile on her face. "That is seriously messed up."

I shrugged, and we both laughed. "So how are things at the flower shop?" I needed to get the attention off me. I wasn't exactly proud of the way I'd been behaving. As a matter of fact, I was angry with myself.

"Really good, busy. I need to get over there shortly. I have a large order for the retirement home. Which reminds me, how is Vi?"

"I'm guessing fine. I tried calling her last night, but there was no answer. She was probably off playing bingo or doing some crafts."

"Sounds like that would be right up Vi's alley." Peggy giggled. "Perhaps I'll stop by and drop off a bouquet of lilies or something. I think she'd like that."

I nodded. "She would love that."

Peggy shoved the last of her muffin into her mouth and then stood up. "Well, I'm off. Oh, and next time he stops in, it's okay to be a little bit nicer, especially if you really do feel that way."

I smiled at my friend. "All right. Have a great day," I called as I watched Peggy walk out the door. She turned and waved before she disappeared out of sight on her way to the flower shop.

I went back into the storeroom and pulled out a small box of books and had just come back out into the store in time to see Thomas' truck pull up out front. I placed the box down on the counter and watched as he sat in his truck for a few minutes, then climbed out.

I took a deep breath. "Be nice, be nice, just be nice," I reminded myself under my breath, then quickly busied myself, pretending that I hadn't seen him at all and went to organizing one of the shelves.

"Hey, Trinity." The little bells above the door jingled.

I turned and smiled. "Hey, good morning." I smiled.

Only he didn't smile back. He had a serious look on his face as he held my casserole dish in his hands. On top of the lid sat the diary.

"Did you read it?" I questioned, stopping what I was doing as I waited to hear what he thought.

Thomas nodded. "I did."

"And? Do you think it was Jed?"

"I'm guessing so. I mean, if I could ask my father, I'd know for sure. He would have probably been just a boy when Jed would have started working for my grandfather. How much of the diary did you read?" he questioned.

"Well, I skipped a few parts. Well, many parts. After all, it is my aunt, and I really did feel like I was invading her privacy." I shrugged.

"You really should read it…all of it."

What more was there that I could possibly need to know? I had lived through the exact same feelings when Thomas had walked out on me. I looked at Thomas, at the strange look on his face. It was like he wanted to tell me something, some huge secret, but I knew my aunt. Sure, she had never told me about her younger years, but that didn't mean I didn't know her.

"Why are you being so insistent? What it that you are implying?" I asked, placing the dish and book down on the counter and crossing my arms in front of my chest.

"I just think that before you go off asking Vi about the things in this diary, you should read the entire journal. It may open your eyes a bit, about many things."

"I've read as much as I need to. I think I know my aunt, Thomas. She'd tell me anything I'd want to know," I bit out. "I certainly don't need to go snooping through her most private thoughts."

Thomas turned away from me, as if he were

keeping some sort of secret from me that I really should know. "Okay, fine, suit yourself."

The room grew quiet, and the tension once again creeped between us. It was different than the tension from the other night at his place when he'd approached me at the counter in his kitchen. This tension was full of coldness instead of heat.

"Will you be doing any work out front today?" I asked quietly, trying to change the tone of the room, while wishing that we really could put our past behind us and sort out some form of a new normal.

"Not today. I have other things I need to take care of." I watched as he moved toward the door. He placed his hand on it and stopped, his tense shoulders beginning to relax.

"I'll come by after the funeral. Friday work fine?" he said, looking down at the floor, then turning his eyes toward me, both full of pain and hurt.

It was in that moment that, once again, I'd been on edge, and my tone hadn't changed. I was still barking at him. Then I heard Peggy in my mind, telling me to be nice. I let out a breath. It wasn't him holding onto to the past; it was me; I was holding onto anger that I'd felt years ago and was using it to push him away from me. Problem was I had thought that I was long over that anger. I wasn't being fair to him or to myself.

"Friday is fine," I said, my tone a little softer this time. "I'll see you tomorrow as well."

His eyes met mine, a little shock in them at the fact that I was going to be at his father's funeral.

"I'll see you later." He nodded, then slipped out the front door.

CHAPTER 11

Thomas

I followed the GPS in my truck out into a part of Willow Valley that I had never ventured. When I was a kid, there was nothing here but empty fields. Now as I drove down the road, a few small subdivisions lined the street. I could already see the retirement home in the distance. I pulled into the visitors parking and slid into a parking spot, cutting my engine.

I hadn't planned on coming out here. I'd planned to go visit Jed in the hospital, but when I'd called earlier to see if I could come and visit him, they'd advised me to call his son. Jack was more than happy to hear from me and apologized for not calling sooner. He let me know that his father had decided to move into the retirement home upon release. So, he had obliged the old man and got him settled in. During our conversation, he did mention he was rather worried about his father and hoped that perhaps a visit from me might help lift his spirits.

I wandered through the halls in the direction the front desk had given me until I came upon Jed's room. I looked in through the door. He lay in bed, on his back, staring up at the ceiling, looking rather depressed. I shook my head. Jack had also warned me that his father's spirits weren't as they had been in the past and that I probably should prepare myself.

"Knock, knock," I called. I expected Jed to answer, but he didn't even turn his head. He just lay there staring up at the ceiling.

I frowned to myself and stepped inside of his room. "You up for visitors, old man?" I called out, smiling to myself because I knew that would get his attention.

"Who the hell wants to visit this old man?" he called out.

I smiled, removed my hat, and proceeded to enter the room and sit down in a chair by the window. "Me. That's who! How are you doing?" I asked, placing my hat down on the table.

"Well, fine I guess, now that I've decided that I want to die."

I let out a laugh that came straight from my gut and shook my head. "Why is that?"

"Well, I fractured my wrist, and you know as well as I do that if a horse broke its leg bad enough, it would be put down. I just don't understand why I'm even still here."

I let out another loud laugh. "Jed, for as long as I've known you, you've been a miserable old bugger. I'm glad to see you haven't changed! All this talk of dying though, it's got to stop. Jack is worried."

"It's the truth!" Jed said, turning to look my way. "You, more than anyone, should have learned that by now."

"Yep, you're right, it is the truth. Only there is one problem," I said, leaning forward.

"Yeah? What's that?"

"You're not a horse," I answered. "Now, don't let a fractured wrist hold you back. Keep your spirits up because you'll be back to normal in no time, and we won't be able to keep you down!"

"Oh, what do you know anyways. All you young kids are the same," Jed said.

"We know absolutely nothing. But I do know one thing. The reason I came here today was because I figured I might be able to give you a reason to live."

"If you say Jack, I'll tell you right now—"

I held my hand up, stopping him. "It isn't Jack."

Jed took one look at me and shook his head, then waved his large hand in my direction. "If it isn't my son then what is it?"

"What if I told you that the love of your life was here?"

Jed looked at me. "Don't be ridiculous. My Elizabeth has been gone for twelve years. No matter how bad I might want her back, she isn't coming."

I got up from my chair and sat down on the edge of the bed and looked at Jed. "I'm not speaking of Elizabeth," I said, my voice low.

"Well, that is the only love I have."

"No, it's not," I said, matter of fact.

Jed didn't say anything. He just looked at me, a question in his eyes. Then he pushed himself up a little. "Ah, you damn kids. You don't know what you're talking about half the time."

"Jed, I do. You left her, exactly the way I left Trinity. Then, over the years, you met and married your rodeo queen and had a son. Then she left you. I know you, Jed. You've never thought that you deserved love, not only because you told me that a million times but because that is exactly the way I've felt most of my life. You could never quite get it through your head that she loved you."

"Lunchtime!" We heard a woman sing from the door.

We both looked in the direction and saw a young girl carry in a tray and place it on the table beside Jed's bed.

"I'm not hungry," Jed grumbled.

"Mr. Hawkins, you don't want to miss this meal. We've got clam chowder and chocolate cake for dessert," the young girl replied smiling at him.

When Jed didn't respond I smiled at the young girl. "You can leave it here. I'll make sure he eats his lunch." I winked.

She nodded, set the tray on the bedside table, and made her way back to the door and continued her way the down the hall. I looked back to Jed, who sat there staring at me. "Now back to what you were saying. What makes you think you know all this?"

"I read all about you. Now, eat up your lunch, and then I will take you for a walk and show you what I mean."

"I told you…I'm not hungry…and I'm not going anywhere. I'm going to lay here in peace. Now, if you don't mind, I'd like to have some time to myself."

Jed refused to look my way. I sat there for a couple of minutes more, then I got up and made my way to the door, looking back at him, but he still hadn't looked my way. Jed was still as stubborn as ever, and if he wasn't willing to come with me, that was okay. There was more than one way to do this.

I wandered down through the halls of the retirement home, following one of the employees to the crafts room. "She's normally in here in the early afternoons. She really enjoys working on her floral arranging, and sometimes she works on her needlepoint, or she reads. Just depends on her mood," Florence, the girl who'd been asked to take me to see Vi, said. "You say you're an old friend of her niece, Trinity?"

"That's correct. I just came into town and heard she was here. So, I thought I'd stop by and see how she was doing."

"Not a problem, sir," she said, pushing a door open. "Yep, there she is, over by the window." She nodded toward where Vi was sitting.

"Thank you so much."

I entered the room and walked over to where Vi sat. "Hello, Vi!" I said sitting down across from her.

She looked up from what she was working on, a surprised look on her face. "Well, if it isn't young Thomas Jenkins. How are you doing, dear?" Vi asked.

I was surprised that she recognized me after all these years.

"I'm doing well, Vi. How are you? I see you've decided to retire," I said, looking around the beautiful sunroom.

She smiled and placed her needlepoint down on her lap. "I have. My Trinity is now running the store. Have you stopped by to see her yet?"

I nodded. "I have. She's still as stubborn as ever." I smiled. "Although, I'd expect nothing less." I chuckled.

"I must talk to her about that. There is no need to be so stubborn. Is she doing okay? I worry about her. I ask, but she tells me not to worry."

I nodded and smiled. "No need to worry. She is doing fine."

"Good. You are right, you know, with her stubbornness. I never know if she is telling me the truth. You were always a good boy, though, and I know if there was something wrong, you'd tell me."

"I would, although that would mean she'd need to tell me, and since she is barely speaking to me, it makes it difficult." I laughed as Vi giggled.

"You know, it's too bad you and Trinity never stayed together," Vi said, looking down at the needlepoint that she had in her lap. "I always thought that you would have made an amazing pair. I always thought a lot of you, Thomas."

I grew quiet, then nodded, swallowing hard. I'd thought of that myself, often, of what might have happened had I stayed in Willow Valley, or if Trinity had come with me. Those thoughts haunted me for many nights while I'd been on the road. They still haunted me today.

"So I'm sure you're wondering why I've stopped by."

Vi nodded. "A little bit, yes. My first thought was that you were here to ask for my Trinity's hand, but that was a long time ago. I lose track of time sometimes."

"That's okay. It was a long time ago. I'm not here because of Trinity. I'm here because there is someone that I'd like you to see. An old friend."

"Oh?? Who would that be?"

"Vi, the other night, I found your diary," I said, swallowing hard, unsure of what reaction I would get.

"Oh, is that so," she said, looking over at me.

I nodded. "Yes, you wrote about Jed Hawkins. Of course, you may not remember. It was a long time ago. After all, you were just a young girl."

"Oh, I haven't thought of him in years," she said, her eyes taking on a far-off look as she stared out the window, lost in her own thoughts. After a while, she looked over at me and shook her head. "Thomas, Jed moved away years ago. I've not seen him since."

I smiled. “Vi, how would you like to take a little walk with me?” I questioned.

“Where are we going?” she asked as she looked down to the needlepoint that sat in her lap.

“To see your old friend.”

She bundled up her needlepoint and placed it into a basket that sat beside her. “I guess we could do that. Now tell me, who is it we are going to see?”

I held my arm out for Vi, and she laced her small arm through mine. We slowly made our way down the hall and to Jed’s room. We stopped just outside before she had a chance to see who was inside, and I looked at her.

“Vi, I’ve brought you to see Jed Hawkins.”

Vi slowly lifted her head and met my eyes. “I have nothing to—”

“Now, Vi, as you said, it’s been years. Please, he’d like to see you.”

Vi looked around. I could tell she was annoyed, but she’d be even more annoyed if she knew I’d lied to her. “Well, you go in first,” she said, crossing her arms.

I couldn’t help but smile, and then I nodded, instantly recognizing where Trinity got her stubbornness from. “Sure thing. Now don’t be like your niece.” I winked.

I walked into the room, Vi, behind me, and stopped just inside.

"I thought I told you I'd like some time…"

Jed stopped as I stepped to the side so he could see Vi. The instant their eyes met, he grew quiet. I looked down to Vi, who stood there. I wasn't sure, but I thought I saw a slight smile line her lips.

"Vi? Is it really you?" Jed asked, clearing his throat. "Or is this jerk playing some kind of joke on me."

"Yes, Jed, it's me," Vi whispered, looking up at me with a soft smile and the hint of a tear in her eye. "Would you help me over to sit down," Vi asked me.

I took her by her hand and led her over to the chair I'd been sitting in earlier, and then I stood off to the side, allowing them some time to get reacquainted. At first, it seemed a little tense, but the more they talked, it was almost as if all the time that had passed hadn't mattered. Soon they were laughing and joking, and before I knew it, they were well into a conversation, and the next thing I knew, Jed asked me to help him up. Before I left, I walked them both down to the garden and left them together under a beautiful old willow tree. As I left to go to my truck, I turned to take one more look at them, and to my surprise, they were already holding hands.

CHAPTER 12

Trinity

I'd never been so happy to see a day end as I was tonight. Since Aunt Vi had retired, I had decided to start up the weekly book club again, meaning that Wednesday nights I wouldn't be done with my day until almost nine. To top things off tonight, I'd forgotten to lock the door after Peggy had left, and I ended up with a surprise shopper who decided to take their time.

I'd showered and changed and had just sat down and began relaxing, a hot cup of tea at my side, when the phone rang. I frowned, wondering who it could be, just as Luna jumped up into my lap and rubbed her head against my chin.

"Hello," I answered.

"Hey, Pet. How are things?" a familiar voice asked.

"Aunt Vi! How are you? Are you enjoying the new place?" I asked, excited to finally hear from her. I'd been meaning to go and visit, but with everything that had gone on in the past couple of weeks, I hadn't found the time.

"Oh, it's wonderful, dear. I've been doing my crafts and getting lots of sunshine and rest. They have beautiful gardens to walk in, and so many things to do, it's hard to keep up."

"That sounds wonderful. How is the food?"

"It's definitely not my own home-cooked meals, but it will do."

"Well, I plan on coming for a visit soon. I do have a few things I can bring for you if you'd like. Including groceries so you can cook up your own things." I almost laughed at the thought of why I'd made the chicken and dumplings I'd just frozen. "I actually just made your chicken and dumplings."

"Oh, I haven't had that in ages. Will you bring me up some."

"Sure, I will," I said. "What else have you been up to? Have you read anything decent lately?"

"They don't have much of a selection here yet.

They are still working on building up the library. Perhaps you could bring me a couple of my favorites?"

"Of course, I can. I can bring you the new Danielle Steel, perhaps a couple Nora Roberts, and I should have the new Colleen Hoover as well."

"That would be wonderful. That should hold me over until they get their act together with the library."

I couldn't help but giggle at the annoyance in her voice. I'd imagine she could have stalked the library herself at one point if given the task. When I focused back to our conversation, I'd noticed Aunt Vi had grown quiet. "What else?" I asked.

"Trinity, I wanted to talk to you about something," Aunt Vi said, her voice taking on a serious tone.

"Oh, are you sure everything is okay?" I asked, suddenly worried that something might be wrong and that she hadn't been able to say anything. Or perhaps her health wasn't good, and she wasn't feeling well.

"Trinity, I had a visitor today."

"Oh? Who?" I asked.

"Thomas Jenkins."

My jaw clenched tightly. How dare he go out there and visit my aunt, I thought to myself. The audacity! I could feel the irritation building inside of me, and I reminded myself to have a talk with him when I next saw him. I needed to give him a piece of my mind and tell him not to bother my aunt. I let out a breath and did my best to calm myself, remembering that he wasn't the one on the other end of the phone. Aunt Vi had done nothing wrong.

"Ah, that was nice of him to stop by," I lied through clenched teeth. "Hope you had a nice visit." It was like my mouth was on autopilot, spewing out words I didn't mean.

"Has he been by to see you?"

I closed my eyes. "Yes, he's been here. His father passed away, so he came home to sell the ranch, that's all. After that is done, I am sure he will be gone. Good riddance."

"Yes, that was what he said. It's too bad about his father. You know, Trinity, I've been thinking that perhaps the two of you should get together, try to work out some of your differences. Perhaps he could do some of the work around the bookstore that's been needing to be done," she said, clearing her throat. "Lord knows the place could use a little love."

I pinched the bridge of my nose. "Well, Aunt Vi, he has been by, and he has been doing some work around here. It was somewhat of a miscommunication, to be honest."

"A miscommunication?"

"Yes," I said, stroking Luna's head. "He made me angry, so I shoved a list at him. I didn't expect him to actually do any of it."

"Wonderful, dear, and..." She practically ignored everything I'd just said.

"And what? I took him some food, and I'm going to the funeral tomorrow."

"Well, that is good. I'd expect nothing less, but really, Trinity, I think you should—"

"Aunt Vi, Thomas and I..." I grew quiet. I wasn't sure what I wanted to tell her; all I knew was that I didn't want any interference from anyone. We were worlds apart; he still had rodeo in his blood, and I knew he had no plans to stay in Willow Valley. My home was here, and I had no desire to leave, so to be honest, there really was no point in trying to reconcile our differences.

"Dear, I know, he broke your heart."

"Yes he did."

"But that was years ago."

"May have been, but, to be honest, I'm not sure I'm over that just yet. The day he walked in, I was so shocked and surprised to see him standing in front of me that I wasn't sure how to react. It's been years, and he still looked the same. It was like I was transported back through time."

"I understand, but try and keep an open mind okay."

"An open mind? Right, so I can get hurt again? No, thank you." I frowned. As if Aunt Vi should talk. She had done the same thing all those years ago, according to her diary.

"Trinity, it's time to stop being so stubborn. People do change. Sometimes, you just need to give them a chance to prove it."

I closed my eyes, it was on the tip of my tongue to ask her what happened between her and Jed and explain that I had read her diary, when she let out a yawn.

"Sorry, Pet, I need to get to bed. I have an early-morning gardening class to take and need to get some rest. It was a very long and exciting day. Will I see you soon?"

"You will," I said. "Love you, Aunt Vi."

"Love you too, Pet."

I hung up the phone, wondering what she could have meant by it being an exciting day, as her comment about Thomas stopping by to visit ran through my mind. He'd better not have said anything to her about the diary. I placed the phone down on the table and picked up my tea and took a sip, then I leaned back against the couch and closed my eyes. Tomorrow was the funeral. I wasn't looking forward to going, but I knew that once it was over, Thomas would sell the ranch, and he'd be gone for good, and my life could get back to normal.

The morning started out hot and sunny, and I found it was a rather warm day for mid-September. I'd gotten up, made breakfast, gotten dressed, and then made my way down to the store and posted a little note in the front window, notifying anyone who stopped by to come back a little past two.

I left Luna lying in the chair in the front window and decided to walk down to the church, meeting up with Peggy along the way. We made it just in time for the ceremony, and once it was over, we all went out into the small cemetery beside the church. Mr. Jenkins was being buried beside his wife, which wasn't that far from where my parents had been laid to rest many years ago. As we followed behind the crowd, Peggy and I stopped at their graveside. I took a quick minute and walked over so I could remove any dead flowers.

"What happened to them?" Peggy asked.

"Oh, Dad was killed in a ranching accident shortly before I was born, and Mom passed away in a car accident just outside of Willow Valley when I was five. She was hit head on by a drunk driver."

"So, you've lived with Vi since then?"

I nodded. "Yes. I barely can remember my mom,

but that is okay, Aunt Vi has been like a mother to me all these years," I said, stepping back away from the headstone and looking down at their names and softly smiling, just as Thomas walked by us with the minister.

We both watched after them. Thomas walked beside the minister, his head low, not acknowledging either of us. As I stepped onto the walkway, Peggy leaned into me and whispered, "Thomas looks pretty wrecked. Perhaps you should go stand with him during the burial."

I nodded, and together we began walking over to the graveside where Mr. Jenkins was going to be buried and looked at Thomas. His eyes were red, and he looked more than exhausted. He'd gone through this entire ordeal alone, and even though his relationship with his father had never been that great, it was still his father. I could tell he was hurting, and no matter how I felt toward him, I hated seeing him this way.

"We should get over there," Peggy said, pulling on my arm and guiding me through the crowd.

It was only a matter of minutes until the minister began speaking in a quiet voice. I felt Peggy nudge my shoulder, and I slowly made my way around to where Thomas was standing and slipped in beside him, thinking of what Aunt Vi had said to me last night, to stop being stubborn. He needed someone, and there was nothing wrong with me being his friend. He kept his hands crossed in front of him and his head down, not making eye contact with anyone, his body visibly tense.

I waited until the minister led us in prayer, so everyone's heads were bowed, before I reached over and slid my hand into his. Instantly, I felt his large warm hand wrap around mine, and he turned his head slightly to look at me. Then, as if my touch was making him more comfortable, his body visibly calmed and relaxed.

"Thank you," he mouthed, then softly smiled before he looked back down at the ground in front of him.

We stood that way until the service was over and his father's casket was lowered into the ground, followed by another prayer. I knew everyone there had their eyes on us and I was happy when the crowd began to break. The minister invited everyone back into the church for a small lunch. As the people made their way back into the church, soon it was only Thomas and me in the cemetery. He just stood there, holding onto my hand, staring down at the casket that had been lowered into the ground.

"Are you ready to go in?" I asked quietly.

Thomas looked up at me and looked around. He seemed surprised that we were the only two still outside. "I was so deep in thought; I didn't notice everyone had gone." He turned away from me for a moment and wiped his eyes.

"They just went inside to have some lunch. Are you hungry?" I asked softly. I waited for a response, but one didn't come. I gave him a moment, then went to tap him on the shoulder, but before I could, he turned back to face me. Without a word, he wrapped his arms around my waist and pulled me against him, hugging me tightly. At first, I was shocked, but he didn't let me go, instead he just held me tight. I slowly brought my arms to his shoulders and returned the hug.

As he let me go, I figured we would head back into the church, but he leaned in and gave me a small kiss on the lips, and the second his lips touched mine, I felt a surge of excitement flood my body.

Before I could stop myself, my lips slowly moved against his, then, as if someone had kicked me, I pulled myself away. Now after that small kiss, I knew every feeling I had ever felt for him was all still there, and so was every reason why I'd never been with anyone else.

"I really should be going," I whispered, looking around to make sure that no one else had seen what had just happened. The last thing I needed was to have rumors running throughout the town about us.

"Trinity, please…stay with me."

I shook my head and turned away from him, bringing my hand up to my bottom lip.

"I need you," he said in a low tone.

I turned around and met his eyes. One look at him told me that he wasn't asking because of what had just happened; he was asking because he truly needed me.

I hesitated for a moment, unsure as to whether I should, but then I heard Aunt Vi's words in my mind. *"It's time to stop being so stubborn. People do change."*

"Please," he begged, holding out his hands toward me. "I've faced my entire life alone. Now all of this. I don't want…I can't do it anymore."

His words hit my heart, and I looked down to his large hands that he held out for me to take. Before I could stop myself, I slipped my hand into his. He looked down at me, and with tears in my eyes he pulled me into him. Wrapping his arm around my shoulders, we walked back toward the church together.

CHAPTER 13

Thomas

The old ranch house probably hadn't seen this type of activity since my mother's passing, I thought to myself as I glanced out the front window. The driveway was full of cars, and the living room was full of people from town who had come to spend their afternoon sharing memories of my father. I glanced over to Lyle, who stood talking with one of the other ranch hands from Darling Ranch and was about to make my way over to them when I heard my name.

I turned around to see Brooke standing behind me, a soft smile on her face. "Hey, Brooke. Thank you so much for coming. Mom and Dad would be thrilled you stopped by. They always loved the diner and bakery."

"You're welcome. I can't begin to tell you how much your parents are going to be missed. I mean, it was hard not seeing your mother for a while, but your father still came by, but it will be all new for me once again. For the first time in my entire life, I won't be serving your dad his favorite breakfast any longer. It makes me sad to think that."

"I know. He sure did love it there," I murmured, remembering all the times my parents had gone into town just for breakfast when I lived here. From what I remembered, it had been his Sunday treat. It was a couple of hours in the morning that he got away from the ranch with my mom where he could leave some responsibility behind and just relax. "Thanks for coming, Brooke," I said, leaning in and giving her a hug. "It's been good to see you, and I appreciate the support, and the mushroom quiche that you dropped over as well."

"Well, it was the least I could do." She smiled up at me and placed her hand on my bicep. "If you need anything, a shoulder, a friend, you know you can stop by anytime. My door is always open."

I glanced around the room and caught Trinity watching us, a look of what appeared to be jealousy washing over her face. It was a look I'd seen a long time ago—years ago—over the same person I was speaking to now. I walked Brooke over to the door and said good-bye, seeing her out, and then turned back to the crowd. Trinity came walking out of the kitchen with a cheese tray in one hand and a plate of crackers in the other. I watched as she placed them down on the large dining room table and spoke to a couple I recognized. She smiled and laughed, then made her way back into the kitchen, not once glancing in my direction.

"Thomas, I'm so sorry to hear about your father," I heard a deep voice say, and turned to see Connor Darling, the new owner of the Darling Ranch. Connor's parents had retired and had left the ranch to him. From what I'd heard from Lyle, this was the first year that ranch had turned a decent profit. Connor and his young bride had just moved onto the property in the spring, and Connor was hell-bent on making it the most profitable and largest ranch in all of Willow Valley.

"Hey, Connor, thank you."

"Mom and Dad wanted to stop by, but after such a long drive back, Dad wasn't feeling too well."

"It's not a problem. I know they send their respects. I did see them earlier today at the funeral, so you tell him not to worry about it," I said, shaking his hand.

"Will do. Look, I know you're probably not sure yet

about what you are planning to do with the place, and now is probably not a good time to ask, but if you're looking to re-home those cattle out there, I have room and would be willing to pay a hefty sum for them. Same with the horses."

It was just like Connor to start trying to negotiate some sort of business deal. Lyle had warned me, which I appreciated; however, it wasn't necessary as I'd gone to school with Connor. He hadn't changed. Plus, I knew his father had been the same in his day. The Darling family name had come up more times at my father's dinner table than I cared to remember, and I knew my father would probably cringe that I was even thinking of selling the animals to him.

I cleared my throat. "I'll have to let you know," I muttered. "Not sure what I am going to do just yet." I was still debating on weather I wanted to sell or try and make a go of it here. I glanced across the room at Trinity. To be honest, I already knew the answer.

As if she could sense I needed out of this conversation, she looked over at me then walked right over and waited by my side, standing there with her arms crossed in front of her. "Excuse me for interrupting, Connor, but Thomas, could I see you for a moment?" she asked.

"Sure. What is it? What do you need?"

"Could I see you in the kitchen?"

"Well, I guess that is my cue. Thanks for coming, Connor, and thank you for the offer. I'll let you know once I decide." We shook hands, and then I followed Trinity into the kitchen. "What's going on?" I questioned.

Trinity smiled at me. "Nothing. I could tell from the look on your face that you wanted or possibly needed out of that conversation, so I thought I'd come save you."

As I looked at the sparkle in her eyes, I realized I'd had no clue when she had become this beautiful. I mean, she was always gorgeous to me. It just seemed that now she was even prettier. I smiled.

"You have no idea how happy I am that you did that. I also want to thank you for all that you are doing here today. It's been a huge relief off my shoulders to have someone making sure all the food is full. But on that note, I didn't want you here to work."

Trinity looked around the kitchen and walked over to the counter where the large slab cake was. She picked up the knife and sunk it into the soft icing, cutting the cake into tiny squares. "It's not a huge deal. Really, I like keeping busy." She shrugged.

She pulled the knife from the cake and proceeded to cut it again, this time her eyes meeting mine. We both stood there not saying anything, just looking into each other's eyes. Silence fell around us, and suddenly, it felt as if we were the only two in the entire house. I was just about to lean in and kiss her when a loud eruption of laughter came from the other room, interrupting the silence that had fallen between us. Her eyes immediately left mine and she focused on slicing the cake.

"I've got to get this cake out. I'm sure people are waiting," she said quietly as she pulled the platter closer to her.

I wanted her to turn back to me, to meet my eyes again. However, she was focused, and I just stood there watching her as she cut and placed the squares onto the platter. I cleared my throat. "This might be forward of me, but I'd love it if you'd stay tonight. It would be nice to spend the evening with someone, have dinner. It gets lonely out here."

Trinity glanced at her watch, and then looked around the room. I could tell she was feeling a little uneasy, which was not my intention at all.

"It would be nice to just relax and watch a movie. No ulterior motive here. Perhaps have a coffee out on the front porch after," I said, holding my hands up. "I promise, just two old friends, relaxing and sharing an evening together."

"Oh… of course. I didn't think…" She swallowed hard. "Well, I guess I could, but I should head back into town to the store and make sure that Ava is okay first."

"You do whatever you need to. Or you can always call her. I do have a phone," I said, nodding to the old beige phone that hung on the wall.

A small smile fell onto Trinity's lips at something I said—an actual smile. As my eyes washed over her face, I could see the hint of blush in her cheeks.

"I guess I could do that," she said, looking into my eyes. "I could even cook us dinner."

"Well, I'd be up for that, provided it isn't chicken and dumplings." I smirked.

Trinity looked to me then dropped her eyes to the floor. "Still don't like them?" she questioned, a serious look on her face.

"In case you didn't notice, I hate them."

I watched as Trinity smiled again. "I'm sorry about that. I seriously didn't expect you to eat them. I was sort of shocked that you did. I thought that perhaps over the years you'd grown to liking them, until you started sweating and going pale."

I couldn't help but laugh. "What do you say, will you stay for a bit tonight?"

Trinity nodded, her cheeks pink. "I will."

I nodded, smiling at her answer. "Well, I better get back out there," I said, turning and heading toward the living room. I looked back over my shoulder in time to see Trinity watching me as I walked away. I couldn't help but wink at her. I was really excited to spend some time alone with her. I just hoped that it didn't end in an argument. I took in a deep breath, turned my attention back to the living room and all the guests, and went about accepting condolences about my father.

CHAPTER 14

Trinity

I'd driven all the way back into Willow Valley my stomach in my throat at Thomas's question. I wasn't sure I should have agreed to go back tonight. Thomas was probably feeling lonely, and after all the time I'd spent protecting my heart over the years, I wasn't sure if this was a wise idea or not. I pulled into my small driveway and entered in through the back door, placing my purse down on the small bench. I made my way to the front of the lower level to find Ava straightening up some shelves, while Peggy sat in the front chair with Luna on her lap, looking through a couple of books.

"Trinity, I didn't expect you to be back before the store closed," Ava said, turning in my direction and getting down off the small step stool.

"I said I'd be back in time for you to leave at five. You've done me a lot of favors this week." I shrugged, looking over to Peggy, who sat there studying me. I knew from the look she was giving me that she knew something had happened.

"Thanks, Trinity. I appreciate it," Ava said, pushing the stool back in beside the bookshelf and grabbing her bag from behind the counter. "I'll see you tomorrow morning?" she asked before walking out the front door.

"Yep, it's your day to open." I smiled.

"I'll be on time, bright and early! See you later. Bye, Mrs. Hollis."

"You too, Ava. Have fun tonight," Peggy replied.

We watched as Ava stepped outside, pulling the door shut behind her and heading off in the direction of home. I walked over and turned the open sign to now read closed and locked the front door.

"Well? What happened?"

I walked around behind the counter and began my closing routine. "Well, shortly after you left, I made the mistake of going over to Thomas while he was in the middle of a conversation with Connor Darling. Thomas just looked uncomfortable, and I figured I'd help him out by putting an end to the conversation."

"And?"

"Well, he ended up asking me to come by tonight for a movie," I said, opening the cash drawer and pulling the receipts out. "And stupid me offered to cook dinner," I said, placing my face in my hands.

"Are you going to go?" Peggy questioned.

"I don't know. I'm not sure. I did see him talking with Brooke earlier. She sure was flirting up a storm, from the looks of it," I muttered. "I just fear he is lonely, and I'm not sure I want to be on the receiving end of that."

"I'm sure he is lonely. I think, though, that instead of thinking the worst, you just might want to accept that fact that maybe he might want something familiar or that was familiar in his surroundings right now. He's lost everyone. I know I was that way after my Greg died," Peggy said, getting up and placing Luna down in the chair and making her way over to me.

"Perhaps you're right."

"I know I am. Plus, it might give you guys a real chance to clear the air. I know you have been struggling since he came back into town with so many unanswered questions."

I nodded and smiled at my best friend. "You're

right."

"I know I am," Peggy said, hugging me. "Now, get ready and go enjoy your date."

I looked at Peggy and smiled. "Very funny."

She couldn't help but laugh as she grabbed her light jacket off the back of the chair. she'd been sitting in. "I should get going anyways. I need to place my flower order tonight."

"Sounds good. And, if I am going to go tonight, I better get all this taken care of. I'll see you tomorrow morning?" I questioned.

"Yep, around nine?"

"Sounds good." I walked Peggy over to the door and locked it once again as Peggy left, then I went about closing the small bookshop.

I'd returned out to the Jenkins Ranch a little after seven with a pizza. It wouldn't have been my first choice, but it was an easy one. When I pulled in, the entire driveway was empty, and just as I got to the bottom of the wooden stairs heading up to the porch, Thomas stepped outside. He took the box of pizza from me and welcomed me in with a tired smile. One really good look at him and I noticed that he looked more tired than he had earlier, and I realized that perhaps Peggy was right. Thomas really didn't want to be left alone tonight, and being surrounded by someone familiar was his way of trying to deal with the day. We'd both attacked the pizza, and once that was gone, we sat on the couch together, watching a movie I couldn't even remember the name of.

I remembered when we were younger and had sat on this couch. We'd practically shared the same cushion, and his parents, especially his mother, would constantly try and keep us separated. I could feel the laughter coming on as I thought about one incident where she kept calling me into the kitchen for silly things just to get me off her son, or him off me, however you wanted to look at it.

Now as I looked at him, sitting there across from me, the Grand Canyon could practically fit between us, and no one would ever guess we were once together. Thomas sat on one end of the couch and I on the other, both of us hugging the respective arm. His mother would have something to say about this, too, I was sure—if she were still with us that is.

I shifted uncomfortably in my seat. Since I had gotten here, we had said maybe half a dozen words to one another. I felt that it was now just an unbearable silence that I couldn't take much longer. I cleared my throat, about to say something, when Thomas looked over at me. His eyes said it all; he, too, was feeling the same discomfort.

I swallowed hard and cleared my throat once again. I had only one question on my mind, and I was fighting to keep it in. Yet when I looked over at Thomas, that question came flying out of my mouth before I could stop it. "Why?"

Thomas blinked. "Why what?" He looked at me, confused.

I needed to know the truth about what happened long ago between us. How does a person leave when they love someone? I had felt that maybe it had been me, that perhaps he wanted something more with someone else. I really didn't think he had left me because of his father. "Why did you leave?"

Thomas frowned. "Why did I leave?"

Annoyed, I let out the breath I was holding. "Yes, Thomas, why did you leave?"

I waited as he sat there, surely thinking about the past. I figured it would have been some huge, long explanation, but instead, he shocked me with his answer. "Honestly, I didn't think I was leaving because I thought you would have followed me." He shrugged.

In my mind, that wasn't a substantial enough answer. For some reason, it only made me angry because he was trying to put the blame onto me. He had no idea how his words that night all those years ago had made me feel. They made me feel that I didn't matter, that perhaps the years we had been together had been nothing but a couple passing time until they met their true loves. Instead, he was putting the blame on me.

"That is why," he said, probably expecting me to answer him.

I took a moment to gather the thoughts that were racing through my mind. Then I picked up my glass of water and took a drink, setting it back down on the table. I turned to Thomas. "You know, I would have followed you anywhere."

"But you didn't, Trin. You didn't follow."

Instantly, I could feel my anger flaring. Yep, he was trying to put the blame onto me. "Let me finish."

"Okay, fine, finish," he responded, holding up his hands.

"I would have followed you anywhere, if I thought I was loved and wanted. You told me, and they were your words, I could come if I wanted. If I wanted, Thomas. That wasn't what I needed to hear. You were asking me to move away and leave behind everything I knew as my home, including the only family I had."

Thomas's eyes fell away from mine and focused back on the TV, and we both fell into another silence. He needed to realize the hurt I felt wasn't because I didn't want to be with him, but because I didn't feel that he wanted me there.

Not another word was spoken until the movie was over, and once it was, he simply stood up and left the room. I could hear Thomas in the kitchen putting away the dishes, so I got up and made my way to the door and slipped my shoes on. I grabbed my purse from the hook just inside the front door. There was no point in staying, I thought to myself. "Thanks for the movie," I called.

"No, thank you," Thomas said, coming back into the living room.

I looked at him, expecting him to now have come to some sort of understanding about why I hadn't followed him, yet he still seemed not to understand. I stood there waiting for him to say something, anything, but when he didn't, I pushed the front door open and walked down the three wooden steps and over to my car. I pulled the door open and was just about to climb in the driver's seat when I heard him call my name.

"Trin."

"What?"

"What can I say? I was a stupid kid." He shrugged.

Yep, and he still didn't get it. Fueled more by anger, I climbed into my front seat and started the engine, then I rolled down the passenger window and looked out at him. "You know what, Thomas, you still are."

I pressed on the gas a little harder than I met to, my tires spinning in the gravel, and once I backed off the gas, my tires gained traction and I headed down the driveway away from Thomas, away from bad, hurtful memories, and back into my current life.

I sat at the small table in the front window of The Crispy Biscuit waiting for Peggy to arrive. I was glad Ava was opening the store for me this morning, which she normally did on Thursday morning. After last night, the last thing I wanted to do was be cheerful.

"What can I get for you today, Trinity?" Melinda asked, approaching the table.

"Do you have the pumpkin spiced latte yet?" I smiled, hoping that they had begun getting some of their fall items.

"Ah, let me check with Brooke. I know she ordered some things last week, so they might have come in," Melinda said, pocketing her little order pad in her apron.

"Oh, and Peggy should be here any minute," I called.

I flipped through the Willow Valley Real Estate

booklet, checking to see if Thomas had in fact listed the ranch but could find nothing.

"You're in luck, Trinity. Brooke said they came in. Just give me a few minutes to find it, okay."

"Great, thank you!"

Just then, the familiar sound of those two little bells chimed, and Peggy walked in. She immediately spotted me, smiled, and came over. "How are you this morning."

"Not too bad. You?"

"Doing okay. It's nice to have the day off after this week." Peggy placed her purse beside her and removed her white jean jacket, then looked at me.

"What?" I questioned.

"Well, what happened last night? Leave nothing out. I'm dying to know all about it."

I hated to disappoint Peggy, but there was nothing to tell. After I'd left, I came home, I curled up with the cat, and read for a while before going to bed. "Not much to tell. Thomas is the same way he's always been."

"What do you mean?"

"He's never grown up. He's never accepted responsibility for what he did. He just doesn't understand how he made me feel all those years ago, and to be honest, I don't think he ever will. He tried to blame what happened between us on me. If you can believe that!"

"Well, since I have no clue what exactly happened, why don't you tell me. Perhaps then I can help you?" she said, leaning back against the booth and removing her scarf from around her neck.

Melinda brought over two pumpkin spice lattes and set them in front of us. Each of us took a sip and placed our breakfast order, and then I began telling Peggy all about the past, all about what had happened. She listened intently, never once interrupting, except when breakfast was delivered. When I was finished, I took of sip of my latte and looked over at my friend, who'd just placed her fork down on the table and wiped the edges of her mouth with her napkin.

"What do you think?"

"I've known you for a long time, Trinity. I don't really know how to say this."

"Just say it. Aunt Vi certainly hasn't been gentle about things either," I said.

"What was your aunt's recommendation?"

I smirked. "That I need to stop being so stubborn."

Peggy looked at me and nodded. "Without sounding like Aunt Vi, I'd tend to agree with her. I think you might be overreacting a little bit here."

"Geez, thanks a lot," I said, placing my fork down on the table and looking at my best friend.

"Seriously, I think perhaps you are both at fault. I think Thomas maybe miscommunicated how he truly felt, given all that he was going through at the time, and I think you were reading into his words and not trusting your heart, even then. I think that deep down you know he loved you so much that he'd of given you anything you wanted, and perhaps that scared you, just like it does now. I think it might be time to let the guard down just a little and see what happens," Peggy said.

I didn't want to hear this. I looked around the restaurant avoiding eye contact with Peggy for a moment. I wasn't sure what I was feeling now, but I certainly didn't want to let my guard down.

"What is it?" Peggy asked.

"You know, I miss my old life. The one without Thomas in it. I'll just be happy once he has left Willow Valley for good. The sooner he can get that ranch up and sold, the better off I'll be," I said, swallowing hard.

"You don't mean that."

"Oh, I do. Seriously, the sooner the better," I said, swallowing hard again. Deep in the pit of my stomach, I felt the unease grow at my words. I didn't mean a single word of what I'd just said, but it was better to put the walls up than to allow myself to feel anything toward that man. I'd been doing it for so long, I didn't know how to do anything but.

"Now, what do we need to focus on today for the fall festival?" I questioned.

CHAPTER 15

Thomas

After Trinity left last night, I couldn't sleep. Our conversation hung heavy in my mind. The look of hurt that lined her face as she got into her car had stayed with me, and if I was ever going to get some sleep, I decided that I'd need to clear my mind. So, I'd gotten up and started going over some of the ranch's finances. Statement after statement I'd finally come to find that Lyle had been right. Dad hadn't turned a profit in the last seven or so years; things had just gone downhill after Mom had passed. From what I could see, I had no idea how he'd even managed to keep the lights on. I'd even called Aaron this morning to get his opinion, and he concluded the same as me, that it was probably best for me to sell the ranch. So, after breakfast, I'd come into town to meet with an agent.

I walked into Willow Valley Real Estate and approached the counter.

"Can I help you?" the lady behind the counter asked, not once glancing up from her computer.

"I'd like to see someone about listing a property," I said, removing my hat. "Thomas Jenkins." I held out my hand expecting a handshake, but the woman continued typing.

"Serenity can see you in a few minutes. If you'd like, you can have a seat," she murmured, nodding to the bank of chairs in the small lobby. "I'll let her know you are waiting."

I took a seat in the small lobby and picked up a magazine that sat on the table and flipped through it.

"Mr. Jenkins, Serenity will see you now," the woman behind the desk said.

I got up and made my way into Serenity's office and closed the door behind me. It took about forty-five minutes to go over everything, but once most of the paperwork was finished, Serenity asked if she could come out and photograph the place. I nodded, and we made an appointment for later this afternoon. When I stepped out of her office, her waiting area was full, everyone's eyes turning to me. Some I recognized, some I didn't, but as soon as I saw one woman lean over and whisper something to another, I knew that the word would be getting around Willow Valley before the listing even went out.

I stepped out onto the sidewalk, glad to be out from under everyone's eyes, and decided that while I was in town, I needed to at least try and make things right with Trinity. Even though I had a ton of food in my fridge at home, which I could have easily brought her, I figured the best thing to do was to stop over at The Crispy Biscuit and get her some lunch. I really didn't have any more of a plan than that, but we'd see where things went.

The Crispy Biscuit was busy. Some people ate out on the small patio, and the lineup was all the way out the door for their bakery counter. So, I took my place in line and waited. It didn't take long for the line to start moving, and before I knew it, I was next.

"What can I get for you, Thomas?" Brooke asked, sliding a fresh tray of cookies into the display case.

"I'm heading over to see Trinity for lunch. I don't really have any idea what she likes from here, so any help or insight you have would be appreciated."

"Oh, sure we can help with that," the girl who stood beside Brooke said.

I looked down to her nametag "Well, Melinda, that would be great."

"You can leave it to me, Brooke," Melinda said, grabbing the menu.

"Order whatever it is she likes, and throw in some dessert there as well," I said, putting my full trust into Melinda.

I stepped off to the side and waited, when finally, twenty minutes later, Brooke appeared with a large bag full of food.

"Okay, Thomas, here you go," she said with a smile.

I glanced down at the bill. "You guys are sure Trinity likes all this?" I questioned while reading it over.

"Yep." Melinda took the money from my hand and shoved it into the register.

I smiled, picked up the bag, and headed out into the street and into my truck. I drove over to Bluebird Books and parked my truck out of sight of the front window. I wanted Trinity to be surprised.

I was just about to the door when it flew open and four kids almost ran into me, shouting thank you to Trinity. I looked in through the front window to see Trinity, wide-eyed, watching me as I quickly moved out of the way of the fifth girl, who ran out the door after her friends.

"Careful, girls," I called after them.

"Sorry!" they screamed and continued running down the sidewalk, while I walked into Bluebird Books, closing the door behind me.

"Hi, Trinity."

I watched as she wiped the counter and then hid the cloth. "Hi, Thomas. What are you doing here?"

I slowly approached the small wooden counter and set the bag of food down. "I brought you some food. Before you protest, I will say it isn't funeral food. I stopped over at The Crispy Biscuit and ordered you some lunch. Brooke and Melinda offered some suggestions, so I ordered everything," I said, pushing the bag forward. "I wasn't sure what you would feel like."

Trinity gave me a partial smile, then let out a breath as she reached for the bag and pulled it closer to her. She pulled it open and looked inside, pulling out three different containers and one box and setting them on the counter. At first, she didn't say anything. She just looked down at all the food in front of her and shook her head a small smile on her face. "Is this payback for the chicken and dumplings?" she questioned, looking at all the food.

"No. They said you liked all this." I shrugged, pulling the containers closer to me to look.

"Well, they sure got you good," she said, a smile on her lips as she removed the last container. "

"What do you mean?" I questioned.

"Eggplant lasagna, liver and onions, hot sausage, and pasta, quite the selection. Oh, and strawberry tarts, shortbread cookies, and lemon pound cake."

I laughed. They had at least given him one thing that I loved, and that was the lemon pound cake.

"Thomas, those girls pretty much picked every item on the menu that I have never and would never order in my life. You'd have been better off coming over here with a stack of waffles."

I couldn't help but laugh. Waffles had always been her favorite; I should have known. "I guess they did get me good. I will mention that to the pair of them when I go back there and ask for a refund."

I watched as Trinity picked up a fork and opened the container that held the lemon pound cake, sliding her fork into the cake and taking a bite. "Well, the least you can do is pay for the cake, because it is delicious."

"Well, their joke may not have given me the food you liked, but it did give me a chance to get you to hopefully hear me," I said, grabbing a shortbread cookie and shoving it into my mouth. "Perhaps I'll also pay for the shortbread. They are good too," I said, grabbing another one.

"Thomas, I think we said all there was to say last night," Trinity said as she slid her fork back into the cake.

I shook my head. "No, you left before I had the chance to be able to talk to you. I know you think that I didn't want you with me all those years ago. But, Trin, you were wrong. I was in such a bad place back then, but you have to know that you were and have always been loved and wanted. In fact, if only you knew how long it took me to get over you, or at least over you enough to live some sort of a life without you, you'd know the truth."

"What are you trying to say, Thomas?" Trinity said, dropping the fork into the plastic container and placing it down on the counter.

"You may not believe me, Trinity, but you still are wanted. From the moment I walked back in here, into this store and saw you standing there, I knew my heart still belonged to you."

Trinity turned to look at me, a look of annoyance on her face. "Please, Thomas, I really don't have time for this nonsense today. I have to do some planning for the fall festival, and I need to put up this small shelf for additional space."

"I'll make sure you have time to get all that done.

Hell, I'll even put the shelf up myself if you'd like. But before you kick me out, just please give me a chance to prove how I feel to you."

"Thomas, please…I don't…"

"No, please, just one chance. That is all I ask, just one," I begged, not wanting to hear the word no.

I looked into Trinity's eyes. There was a softness there, one that hadn't been there before, and I was almost sure I could see the walls she'd put up finally maybe beginning to come down. She looked down to the ground, then she stopped, thinking for a moment, then she looked up at me. "Fine, Thomas, one chance. You can take me out tonight."

I almost couldn't believe my ears. In all her stubbornness, she'd agreed. I was thrilled, and I nodded my head. "Okay, I'll see you at say seven. I'll pick you up."

"All right, fine, seven. Now, please, I need to get some work done."

It had been three hours since I'd left Trinity. Since then, I'd returned to the ranch and had welcomed Serenity, showing her around and allowing her to take some pictures of the property. She'd left about an hour later, and I now sat in the dining room trying to figure out what the hell I was going to do about tonight.

"Me and my big mouth," I mumbled while surfing through a list of things to do in Willow Valley on a Friday night. One thing was for sure: not much had changed over the past twenty or so years since I'd left. There was nothing to do then, and it appeared there was nothing to do now.

"I see the lady from the real estate agency was here today?" I heard from behind me and turned to see Lyle shuffle in from the barn.

I nodded. "Yep, I finally made my decision. The ranch is officially up for sale."

"I see. What does that mean for you?" Lyle asked, pulling out a chair across the way from me.

"Not sure yet."

Lyle nodded. "You aren't sure yet? The place is up for sale?" He chuckled.

I shook my head, looking to see what movies were playing in the theatre. "Guess you could say it depends."

"I see. Does it have anything to do with your lady friend?"

I never knew how Lyle did this. He'd asked me that when I was seventeen. I chuckled. "It might. Do they not run the movie night in the park any longer?"

Lyle shook his head. "No, damn kids now a days,

they don't want to sit out in a bug infested park. Hell, they just want to go to the air-conditioned theater. You'd think they'd melt or something."

I chuckled once again. "Do you know if there is still that little private road off Pelican Trail that heads down to the bay?"

Lyle thought for a moment and nodded. "I believe it's still open. At least the last time I'd heard about it, it was."

"That might work," I muttered under my breath. "What will you do, Lyle? Where will you go once this place sells?"

"Oh, I don't know. I may see if someone down at Connor's place needs some sort of help, or perhaps I'll just rent a little place and put my feet up. You know, finally retire."

"Sorry, Lyle. I feel like I've ripped the place out from under you."

"Don't you worry, Thomas. I knew it was coming. It was inevitable, especially now that your dad is gone. I never expected you to keep this old place. Ranching never was your thing. Perhaps had he understood that you'd not of had the relationship you did with him. He wanted you to run his dream, he never thought about the fact that you might not want that for yourself. Anyways, I think I'm going to go out and do a little work on the fences that need repairing."

I nodded and watched as Lyle made his way out the back door. I had no idea what I was going to do. Aaron had asked me to return to his ranch, said he had a position open that I'd be perfect for, yet no matter how much I thought about it, my heart told me that Willow Valley was where I should be.

CHAPTER 16

Trinity

I stood in front of the mirror in my small bathroom, looking at my reflection, wondering what the hell I was doing. I let out a breath, picked up my hair dryer and began drying my hair. Once finished, I shut my hair dryer off, coiled the cord around it, and put it away before running my brush through my hair. Then I made my way into my bedroom. I had given him no instruction as to what I wanted to do tonight. Instead, I was leaving it all up to him. I glanced at the clock, hoping he would have canceled by now. Why had I opened my mouth? I wandered over to the closet and tried to find something to wear. It was hard to pick an outfit when I had no idea where he was taking me. Dancing? Dinner? The movies? Perhaps he was going to cook dinner?

I sifted through my closet and pulled out a pair of my favorite jeans and my favorite flannel shirt. I figured this was my most versatile outfit—dressy enough for dinner in a restaurant, cool enough for dancing, and warm enough for the theater.

I quickly dressed, then slipped my feet into my knee-high boots, and made my way into the kitchen. I reached for a glass and poured myself some water. Then I went over to the window and looked down at the street. There was still no sign of Thomas. Then I glanced to the small clock that sat on the bookshelf. It was almost seven.

I looked around the living room, at the mess it was, and to try and calm my nerves, I began cleaning up. I quickly picked up the dirty dishes, loaded them into the dishwasher, then folded the blanket I normally kept on the back of the couch. Then I wandered down to my bedroom and picked up all the stray pieces of clothing, throwing them into the hamper in the closet. Then I made my bed, something I normally did every morning, until these past few days.

Once I was satisfied, I went back out and checked the front window once again, just in time to see

Thomas pull up. I grabbed my purse, patted Luna on the head, and made my way downstairs in time to meet Thomas at the back door.

"Ready to go?" he asked as I stepped out the back door, locking it behind me.

"Yep. Where are we are off to?" I questioned.

"You'll see," Thomas placed his hand on the small of my back and guided me over to his truck. He opened the passenger door and waited for me to climb in. "Come on, Trin, up you go," he said taking hold of my arm.

I climbed into the truck and got seated, while Thomas shut the door and walked around to the driver's side and climbed in.

"So, where are we going?" I asked again, hoping he would cave.

"You'll see." Thomas grinned as he pulled away from the curb and drove down the end of the street, making a right-hand turn. We drove for a bit, and then Thomas slowed down, almost coming to a crawl before turning off the road into what appeared to be a driveway. We drove a little way until we came to an opening, and once we were in the clearing, I recognized it instantly.

We used to come here when we dated, so we could be alone. The hidden clearing at the edge of Willow Valley Bay, a place I could barely forget, but hadn't been to since. We'd spent many nights down here at the water's edge, on the dock, under the stars.

I could remember feeling every nerve in my body fire as I waited for him to make his first move when we had dated. Now felt no different. Only this time he didn't make a move. Instead, Thomas opened the door and got out of the truck. I watched in the mirror as he walked to the back of the truck and opened the bed cover. What was he doing?

"Come here, Trinity," he called. I looked in the mirror and saw him waiting for me, so I carefully climbed out of the cab and walked around to the back of the truck. He lowered the tailgate, and I was surprised to see a pile of blankets and pillows all laid out, and in the center a picnic basket.

"I racked my brains trying to come up with something tonight. Thought perhaps we'd do movies under the stars, until I found out they stopped that. Then it came to me. I thought we could share a picnic under the stars. If you give me your hand, I'll help you up."

I didn't know what to say. I hadn't expected this. I hadn't expected him to remember how much I loved being out in nature. I looked up at Thomas and smiled.

"Is this okay?" he questioned, meeting my eyes.

I nodded. "It's perfect."

"I'll help you up," he said, slipping his hands around my waist and lifting me up. Instantly, my body shuddered at his touch, and once I was in the back of the truck, I had to calm my breathing a bit. Then he climbed up behind me and guided me to sit down.

I sat down and watched as he, too, took a seat, then opened the picnic basket and pulled out a bottle of wine and two wine glasses, which he had me hold while he found the corkscrew and opened the wine.

I watched as he poured the two glasses and shoved the cork back in the bottle. Then he took his glass from my hand, his fingers grazing mine. "To you," he said, gently clinking his glass against mine, and then we both took a sip.

"So I brought a little spread of cheese and crackers, nothing fancy, but I did grab a couple more pieces of that lemon pound cake for desert."

I couldn't help but smile.

"What?" he questioned.

I shook my head. "Nothing. This is nice," I said, taking another sip of my wine and looking out over the water just in time to see two ducks' land. I hadn't been out here in years. In fact, the last time I'd been out here had been a night I'd been with Thomas.

"Do you remember the night I stole that bottle of wine from my parents to bring out here?" he asked, his eyes dancing at the memory.

I let out a small laugh. "I sure do. I also remember

both of us chugging on the mouthwash afterward so neither of us would get caught."

"I don't think I ever did tell you, but Mom asked me about a month later what happened to that bottle. Apparently, they had bought it for their anniversary. I made up some story about it falling from the cupboard and smashing on the floor when they weren't home." Thomas laughed.

"Yep, Aunt Vi practically cornered me in the kitchen when I got home that night, swearing she could smell wine on my breath. I thought she was going to pull out a breathalyzer the way she was treating me," I said as we both laughed. As the memory of that night replayed in my mind, I began to grow quiet.

"What are you thinking about now?" Thomas asked.

I shook my head and gave him a small smile. "Just about the last time we were out here." I could feel my cheeks heating at the memory.

Thomas nodded and softly smiled back. "I think I remember that night as well," he said, his eyes meeting mine.

We'd come out here after he'd had a fight with his father. I'd snuck out of my bedroom window long after Aunt Vi had been in bed, climbed down the trellis, and met Thomas at the corner, and he'd driven us out here. Just like now, he'd thrown blankets in the bed of his pickup, only that night, we'd ended up underneath them, naked, wrapped in one another's arms.

"So long ago..." I whispered, remembering what it was like to be held in his arms after our first time, our bodies wrapped together, hot, and sweaty. I looked off into the distance. The memory of that night was something I hadn't thought about for a long time and it was pulling at my heart.

"That it was. Although you barely look like you've aged a day. You still remind me of that young, innocent girl I used to bring back here." He winked.

I could feel the heat rise to my cheeks at his comment. "Thank you, and you stole that innocence away from me." I laughed.

We both grew quiet as we sat looking at one another. The heat between us was still there. I knew we could both feel it, and yet it was like we were teenagers again, and neither of us knew what to do with that attraction.

"You know, Trinity, I meant what I said to you earlier today. I wish we could turn back time, do things differently. There have been so many times I wished I could have just told you how I felt, instead of saying the stupid things I said to you."

It wasn't that I didn't feel the same way because I did; I felt it in my soul. I just couldn't let myself get hurt again, but as I looked at Thomas, I knew from the look in his eyes that he meant what he said. There wasn't a hint of a lie on his face. All that was there was pure devotion.

I swallowed hard. "I've thought a lot about you over the years, Thomas. So much so that I became obsessed with following your career for a long time, wishing that I could have shared in your victories and your failures. I was so proud of you when you won the Triple Crown. That must have been something."

"It was. It really was such a special and exciting time, except it would have been better to have someone to share it with."

"If it makes you feel better, I was celebrating with you," I said, taking a sip of my wine. "Or we could celebrate now."

Thomas smiled. "I did one good thing with that money that made me feel great inside. I was able to help my friend, Aaron, and his wife attain their dream of owning a ranch. I met Aaron my third year on the circuit, and he always treated me well, so I gave him a substantial down payment to buy it. In return, I became a part of their family and they gave me a place to live, a place to finally call home. That was where I was living up until I got the call about my father."

"Wow, Thomas, that really is amazing of you to help them out. Are you still planning on riding?" I asked, sipping my wine and taking a bite of a piece of cheese.

Thomas shook his head. “No, sadly, I’m officially retired from the rodeo. Unfortunately, I’ve suffered too many injuries, and that part of my life has been taken from me.”

I worried when he said that. Worried about the kind of injuries he had faced. I’d seen him bucked off a bull a few times. Then I began wondering what he was going to do when the ranch sold. “That must be hard, to have your career taken from you?”

“It is, but you know, I’ve had a pretty awesome life. Well, that part of it anyways.”

“I’m glad, Thomas. Are you doing okay, injury wise?”

“I am now, doc has me on some medications, well a small pharmacy of them, but since I’ve been back here, the pain seems to have subsided. Same with the headaches.”

“I’m glad to hear it.”

“What about you?”

“There isn’t much to tell.” I shrugged.

“There must be something. Who swept in and took their chances with you after I left town?” Thomas questioned.

I shook my head. “No one. I went to night school,

took a couple of courses, and basically just buried myself in the bookstore business."

"So, you're telling me that Jonathon never came snooping around you after I left?" Thomas asked, jealousy lining his voice.

Jonathon had been the only boy in school brave enough to show interest in me while I'd been dating Thomas. Thomas had put an end to that very quickly, making him understand that I was off limits. Had he come around? Of course, he had, but after one date I promptly told him not to bother. It was just too soon. He had listened and soon after that, his family had left Willow Valley. "He tried, but I wasn't ready," I said, sipping my wine.

We both grew silent. I could feel he had something he wanted to say, so I just waited, eating a piece of cheese and sipping my wine, while he looked out over the water.

"Are you okay?" I quietly asked.

"You know, all this loss in such a short time. First, my career, then my father. I've made so many mistakes over the course of my life, and they are one's that I cannot take back. But there is one that I can rectify now, it's not too late for us. We could have another chance."

I didn't know what to say. A huge part of me wanted the same thing. I was just so afraid of being hurt again. I swallowed hard just as thunder rumbled above.

"It wasn't supposed to rain tonight," Thomas said, looking up at the darkening sky. "Looks like we may have to cut the night short."

The sound of loons rang out in the distance, and I felt a couple drops of rain, and then the sky opened. Rain poured down on us followed by a loud crack of thunder and a flash of lightning. Thomas quickly got up and jumped down out of the truck, then turned and took hold of me by the waist and lifted me down.

"Hurry, get inside, before you get soaked," he said as he placed me on the ground. I quickly ran around to the passenger's side and climbed into the truck. I watched through the mirror as Thomas closed the lid on the bed. Then he, too, came and climbed into the cab, rainwater dripping off his face. We both looked at one another and broke out into laughter, just like we would have done when we were younger.

"So much for that!" Thomas chuckled as he started the engine and pulled the truck around.

By the time we turned down Bluebird Avenue, the rain had stopped. Thomas pulled up to my small driveway and pulled his truck in behind my car.

"I'll walk you to the door if you'd like."

I looked over at him, his blue eyes sparkling in what was left of the light. "That would be nice," I said softly.

He smiled, then came around to open my door. We walked slowly to my back door and there we stood.

"Well, you're home."

"I am. Thank you for a wonderful evening." I looked down at the ground. I felt we had so much more to say, and I didn't want the night to end, but I turned away from him and slid my key into the lock, turning it. I just shoved my keys into my purse when I felt his large hands on my arms. I stilled and looked over my shoulder at him. The look in his eyes told me that he too wasn't ready for the night to end. I cleared my throat, "Would you like to come up for a coffee?" I questioned, hoping that Thomas would agree to coming up, even if it was only for an hour. "It will warm us up after that rain."

He didn't answer right away, he just stared into my eyes and I was afraid he was going to say no, but instead, he squeezed my upper arms, sending waves of electricity through me.

"Are you sure?" he questioned.

I swallowed, catching the scent of his cologne as a

gentle breeze blew. He smelled heavenly. "If I weren't sure, I wouldn't have asked," I answered.

His eyes held mine for a moment, then he stepped forward, his body coming into my personal space as he pushed the door open. I stepped inside the small entryway, putting some space between us so I could breathe, and waited for him to close the door. I slipped my shoes off and climbed the back steps up to my small apartment. We were greeted by Luna, who immediately started criss-crossing between my feet, rubbing her body against my legs.

"Hey, Luna," I said, reaching down and picking her up, introducing her to Thomas.

"Hi, Luna," he said, gently rubbing her head with his large hands. Immediately, she began to purr.

"She likes you," I said, shoving her into his arms and leaving the two of them to get acquainted.

I went over to the small kitchen and turned the kettle on and pulled two mugs from the cupboard and watched as Thomas gently placed Luna onto the couch. He then walked over and leaned up against the counter and crossed his arms. We stood in the quiet, both of us looking at one another. It felt weird to have him here again, and for a quick second, I wondered what I'd been thinking when I invited him up.

I gently smiled at him. Only he didn't smile back. He stood there looking at me with such heat and intensity I had to concentrate on my breathing for fear I'd faint. My body was already beginning to respond to his look alone when he surprised me by taking one step and crossed the kitchen, pulling me into his arms, hugging me tightly. As he let me go, he gently cupped my cheek with his large hand, leaned in, and met my lips. The instant our lips touched, my body was on fire, every nerve from everywhere firing.

Instantly, my arms went to his strong shoulders, and I rested them there, my fingers finding the thickness of his hair, just like they'd done when I was younger, as we kissed. His arms went around my waist, one strong hand resting on the small of my back, as the other rested on my hip, his thumb stroking the soft skin of my abdomen under the edge of my shirt as he kissed me deeper.

"I forgot how good you tasted," he murmured between kisses, his tongue washing through my mouth. "How much I missed these lips."

His kiss deepened, and his body rested against mine, pushing me into the counter. I could already feel his arousal as he pressed against me, harder this time as his hands gripped my hips and pulled me closer against him. I let out a soft moan as his tongue swept through my mouth, then his lips danced down the side of my neck.

In an instant, I was transported back to seventeen,

when in my aunt's small apartment, with her in bed, we made out in the living room on the couch one night after we'd returned from the movies. I could still remember how hard he was and how he held onto my hips as I ground myself into him. It had been so intense that he had to keep his mouth over mine, swallowing my moans as I felt myself let go. Almost like now, except for the fact we didn't have to be quiet.

I gripped his shirt as he kissed me harder, then he moved his lips down the side of my neck, then back up to my ear. I let out another moan, louder this time as he flicked his tongue over my earlobe. My body was on fire, he was on fire, and I wanted more; I wanted him. His hands slid down my backside, cupping my ass and gently squeezing as his lips met mine once again. He held me tight, almost afraid if he let go I wouldn't return to him. I pulled at his shirt and led him down the hall to my bedroom.

CHAPTER 17

Thomas
Four Weeks Later

I opened my eyes, familiar surroundings coming into view. The room was still dark, but I could see the hint of daylight through the blinds. I heard the vibration of my phone and grabbed for it, seeing an email waiting for me. Whatever it was could wait, I thought as I felt Trinity's body pressed against mine. I placed my phone down just as Trinity rolled over and placed her arm around my waist. It felt so natural to have her tucked into my side, and I pulled her into my arms.

Ever since the night down by the water, we'd been

inseparable, going out for dinner, working together on the bookstore, or just hanging at her place. I very rarely made it back to the ranch, and this was generally how our dates ended, waking up the next morning, curled up in one another.

Her body was warm as she snuggled into me. I relaxed into the bed and closed my eye. Instantly, my mind went back to last night. We made love for hours, making up once again for lost time, or so it felt. It was almost three when we were finally spent, both of us, lying in one another's arms, exhausted and breathless. I finally felt at home after feeling so lost for so long. I had everything I needed right here, and my soul was at peace.

"You're still here," Trinity mumbled against my chest as she let out a yawn. I wrapped my arms around her. She was so warm and so at home in my arms, I didn't want to let her go.

"I am. I was planning on getting an early start this morning, but then I decided I wasn't going anywhere," I whispered, placing a kiss on her forehead as once again memories of last night invaded my thoughts.

I'd loved listening to her cries as I licked at her nipples, gently rolling them between my fingers. I'd loved watching from below as she bit her hand to silence her cries, while I sucked that perfect little bundle of nerves into my mouth until she came, her legs resting on my shoulders. She was so responsive to me, and I loved making her beg me to stop when right after she'd come down, I started on her again.

I reached down under the blanket and gripped my already hardened cock. Even though I was all geared up again, my entire body felt relaxed, and I knew that right here with her, this was where my heart laid. It was what my life had been missing all these years. I'd been searching for something that had been under my nose the entire time, and I just hadn't realized it until now.

Trinity closed her eyes and lay there, her breathing steady as she fell asleep in my arms, and I, too, closed my eyes, allowing myself to drift back off. I had no idea how much time had passed when I heard my phone vibrate against the table again, and with Trinity still asleep in my arms, I quickly checked to see who had messaged me. Serenity's name appeared. I was about to open the email when Trinity stretched and let out a yawn.

"Morning," she whispered, then sat up and swung her legs out from under the covers.

"Good morning," I said, my hand gently squeezing her side, wishing she was still naked but taking pleasure in how adorable she looked in her tank top and shorts this morning as she slid from the bed. I watched her as she made her way out of the bedroom and into the bathroom. The way her hips swayed side to side as she moved away from me.

I grabbed my phone as I heard the shower start and took a moment to read Serenity's email. There had finally been an offer made on the ranch.

"Just jumping in the shower," I heard Trinity call.

I barely had time to think about anything. Instead, I quickly replied to the email. At first, I'd asked Serenity to keep the listing private and not put a sign up as I wasn't sure what I wanted to do after Trinity and I had gotten together again. She had kept it quiet and did as I asked and now I'd just accepted the offer. I swallowed hard. I had yet to tell Trinity that ranch had even been for sale. I'd planned to tell her right when I listed it, however we'd just gone out for the first time. I'd tried to tell her one afternoon while working in the store, but a customer came in, then I'd hoped to tell her over dinner one night this past week, but instead, I hadn't, but to me that didn't matter because I knew what I wanted. I wanted her.

"Care if I join you?" I called.

"You know where I am." I heard her giggle.

I quickly got up out of bed and headed toward the bathroom when Trinity came out. She came into the bedroom and pulled open her dresser drawer, pulling out a pair of panties and a bra. I couldn't help but go up behind her, place my hands on her bare hips, and pull her back into me, my cock already hard. I kissed her neck, my hand gripping her breast, my thumb running over her hardened nipple. She let out a slight moan as my other hand found its way between her legs and I ran my fingers through her wet center.

"The shower." She moaned.

I couldn't help but chuckle as she squirmed in my arms, while my fingers, slick with her juices, continued to run over her already swollen bud. My cock ached, and I wanted to take her right there, when my cell phone rang. Distracted by the ringing phone, she took the opportunity to wiggle away from me, giggling as she ran to the bathroom. "You know where to find me, you better hurry," she called out.

Annoyed, I grabbed my phone, answering it, determined to get rid of whoever it was in a flash.

"Hello."

"Morning, Thomas. I just got your email."

"Morning, Serenity."

"I wanted to call. I'm glad to see that you are willing to take the offer. I do have a few things I'd like to go over with you regarding this offer, and if you should agree to them, then all you'll have to do is sign some papers."

I listened with half an ear to what she had to say as she read over the details of the offer to me. It sounded somewhat reasonable to me, but then the only thing on my mind was what I wanted to be doing behind that bathroom door as Trinity waited for me.

"Are you coming?" Trinity called out.

I gripped the phone tightly. "I'm in the middle of something right now, but things seem to be okay. Could I come by a little later this morning and go over all the finer details and sign the offer."

"Sounds good, Thomas, see you then."

I smiled and hung up the phone, taking a moment to realize what it was that I'd agreed to. Then I glanced to the bathroom, and suddenly a surge of excitement ran through me at the thought of perhaps starting a new life.

I opened the bathroom door. The room was full of steam, but I made my way over to the shower. I dropped my shorts and pulled the door open to find Trinity.

"Hurry, it's cold." She laughed, looking up at me with that innocent face.

"Give me a second and you'll be warm in no time," I said as I pulled the door closed behind me and met her lips. As the hot water poured down on both of us, I felt her small hand grip my cock. "Turn around."

"What? Why?"

I didn't answer her. Instead, I spun her around in the small space and gripped her hands in mine. I placed both of her hands against the wall of the shower. "Stay like that," I whispered, nipping at her earlobe, and ran my hands down over her breasts, feeling the weight of them in my hands. While still holding one of them in my hand, I gripped my cock with the other and lined myself up at her entrance, pushing my way in. A wave of electricity flew through me at the sound of Trinity's moan as I waited for her to get used to having me there again.

"Oh God, Thomas," she cried as I held myself deep inside of her.

"Shhh, baby. Just stay like that," I whispered, kissing her shoulder.

I gripped her shoulder with one hand and her hip with the other and slowly and deeply pumped into her as the hot water continued to rain down on us. We continued slow and steady, each stroke getting harder. I loved listening to her; the harder I pumped, the louder she got. I reached down between her legs and stroked the swollen little bundle of nerves, making her beg for release.

I pulled her back against me, gently biting and sucking her neck. "Come for me," I moaned into her ear, my own climax building to the point I knew I wouldn't be able to stop. I felt her tighten around me, her body shaking, and the low moan escaping her as I held her tight, my body tensing as well.

We stood there for a moment, her in my arms, as

the hot water showered over us, relaxing our bodies. As I slid myself from her, she slowly spun around, and I wrapped my arms around her, holding her against me.

I placed two fingers under her chin and raised her head up. Lowering mine, I brought my lips to hers and kissed her deeply. "I love you," I whispered.

She kissed me again, and as I pulled away, I thought I saw a glimpse of a tear. "I love you too," she whispered, hugging me.

"Are you coming out now?" I questioned, as I kissed her yet again. I was ready to go collapse on the bed in exhaustion, and I wanted her with me, even though I knew she couldn't because she had to open the store.

"I'm just going to stay here for a few more minutes," she whispered. "I need to wash my hair."

"Okay." I softly smiled.

I was dried and dressed and was just getting off the phone with Serenity once again, when I saw her step out into the hallway, tightly wrapped in a pink towel.

"That was a great way to start the day." She smiled.

"Sure was," I said, sliding my phone into my pocket.

"Who were you talking to so early?" she questioned.

I let out a sigh. I wasn't sure I was ready to tell

anyone yet. Since it had been only minutes, the shock of selling the ranch was something I still had to digest, but when I looked at her, I knew I had to tell her. Things had been going so well that I didn't want to revisit the path we'd been on before. "That was Serenity Bryson over at Willow Valley Real Estate."

Trinity's eyes flew to mine and she got quiet, her eyes reflecting a look I wasn't sure I liked. "You're selling the place?" she questioned. "When were you going to tell me?"

I could already see the tears beginning to well in her eyes. I didn't want her to panic, to start off assuming things without letting me explain to her. I reached out to take her hands in mine, to ask her to give me a chance to explain, but she stepped backward out of my reach.

"When were you going to tell me, Thomas?" she repeated. "How long has it been up for sale?"

"Trinity, I listed it privately the morning we went on our first date. I planned on telling you, but every time I went to mention it something happened and then it slipped my mind. Things were going so well between us, and I hadn't gotten any offers, so I figured there was plenty of time to mention it. I mean it's not a big deal."

"How can you say it's not a big deal?" she cried.

I met her eyes. I could already see the pain reflected in them.

"Because it's not that big of a deal. It just sold this morning. I haven't even signed anything yet. I don't know if there is anything I might not agree to, and honestly, until the offer is signed, it's really not official. I've got to go down to the office this morning."

Trinity stood there, quiet, looking at me, a whole new world of hurt in her eyes. "And then what? Were you just going to pack up and move away?"

"No!"

"So then you've found a new place to move into?" she asked, a slight glimpse of hope in her eyes.

How could I answer that? I hadn't exactly even begun looking for anything. I frowned. I didn't know what to say. She was putting words into my mouth. I could feel the worry building in me. I didn't want to get into an argument with her first thing this morning, especially after what I'd said to her this morning. I could have taken her to a house I'd purchased, and deep in my gut I felt as if it wouldn't matter anyways because she probably wouldn't believe.

"Well?"

I stood there looking at her, trying to form more words while still trying not to have Trinity freak out. I certainly didn't have the best track record with her. In her eyes, I had literally abandoned her when we were younger and hadn't returned. I really didn't know what reaction I'd been expecting from her.

She turned her back on me, and I watched as her right hand went up to wipe her eyes, while her left hand held onto the knot in the towel.

"I think it's time you leave," she whispered.

I was paralyzed. I couldn't move. I didn't want this to end this way. I wasn't leaving Willow Valley, but for some reason, I couldn't seem to find the words to be able to explain anything.

"Trinity, please, just give me a chance to explain."

She shook her head and sniffled. "I've given you plenty of time. Honestly, don't feel bad, there is no need to explain. Really, it's okay. I understand. I should have known better. Now please, I don't have a lot of time. I have to get ready for work, and you need to go and sign those papers."

"I don't need to leave for a bit yet. Please let's talk about this."

"There is nothing to talk about. Like I just said, I should have known better. I should have known you'd do this again. When things are too good to be true, they probably are." Trinity's voice caught and she sniffled, her shoulders shaking. "Please, just go, Thomas, and don't worry about going with me tomorrow to see Aunt Vi. I'd like some space."

Without another word, Trinity walked across the

hall and slammed the bathroom door behind her. I stood there for a moment, then walked across the hall to the door. I was about to knock, to pull her in my arms and comfort her, but instead my heart broke when I heard her sobs coming from behind the closed door. I should have told her I had put the property up. I should have explained to her that I was going to look for a new place, but for some reason, I hadn't. Her loud sobs hit me right in the chest over and over; she was killing me. I walked into the bedroom and grabbed my shirt from the back of the chair and threw it over my head. Then I made my way out into the kitchen where Luna approached and rubbed up against me. I leaned down and pet her head. "Well, Luna, you take care of your mom okay. I fucked up, sweet girl," I whispered as Luna loudly purred. I stood up, looked around the small apartment, and made my way down the stairs and let myself out the back door and headed to my truck. As I approached my truck, it started to blur and my eyes burned. I'd blown it. I didn't know how to fix it.

"So aside from putting on a new roof on the farmhouse, there are no other stipulations. That can be taken out as well, if you agree to a price drop of the cost of the roof," Serenity said as I looked down at the paperwork in front of me, barely seeing a word.

My head ached and my thoughts were still completely focused on Trinity's words that she should have known better. I'd told her I loved her, which was the truth. At this point, I really didn't care what happened with the property. All I cared was having my Trinity back in my arms and showing her, I was still in love with her.

"Thomas, what do you think?"

I blinked and looked up at Serenity. "Sorry, um, I guess a price cut is fine."

"Well, I will get the word over to the buyers then. The Eastons will be very happy. Oh, and they'd like to let you know that the ranch will no longer be called Jenkins Ranch. They have decided to call it Sunset Ranch. They want to make sure that you are okay with the name change."

"Whatever they decide is fine. This old place needs a new life. Where do I sign?"

Serenity turned some documents around. Each page had a sign here tab, and I slowly went through each page, making sure that I had completed them all.

"Thank you…I feel like this was a fast sale for a truly private listing."

"Sure was. Honestly, I'd had a lot of interest in that property over the years, but your father wouldn't even entertain selling. When you came in and said you wanted to list it, I knew it would go rather quickly. Probably would have been gone in the first couple of days had I have been able to put a sign out." Serenity smiled, gathering up the papers and slipping a paper-clip onto them.

"When is the closing date?"

"Ah, looks like the end of next month, unless, of course, you're going to need more time. I know you'll need to arrange to have the animals taken care of."

"Should be fine. I already have something in the words." I muttered, thinking of Connor Darling's offer.

"All right then, you'll be hearing from me as soon as I hear back from them. Now, will you be needing a place to live?" Serenity asked. "There are some nice homes for sale in the area right now."

I thought to myself, feeling unsure of what exactly my path was. "I'll have to get back to you on that. For now, I'm going to say no and head out to the ranch to start getting some things organized."

"Very well. Well, if you do, please do not hesitate."

As I drove back to the ranch, I felt empty. It had been a such a hard few weeks. I'd lost my parents and sold the last part of them that I had. I'd once again lost Trinity. I had nothing, except a pile of cash, and a duffle bag full of clothes. Despite everything going through my mind, I got straight to work when I got back to the ranch. The first thing I did was go inside and call Connor Darling, and then I sat down with Lyle.

CHAPTER 18

Trinity

I had never been so glad to see a Sunday as I was this morning. After everything that happened between Thomas and me yesterday morning, I was so glad to be going out to see Aunt Vi today. It was just the break I needed, and I was looking forward to spending some time out in the gardens with her if it wasn't too cold out.

I slipped from my bed and shoved my feet into my slippers and grabbed my light cotton robe from the end of the bed. My whole body felt heavy, and I had a horrible headache. I wrapped myself in my robe and shivered; it was starting to get much colder in the mornings. I made my way into the living room and turned the gas fireplace on, allowing it to heat my small apartment.

Then I returned to the kitchen, switched the kettle on, and set up my French press. In a matter of minutes, I was greeted by Luna. I smiled down at the tabby cat then reached up into the cupboard and pulled down a can of food, opening it and dumping it into Luna's bowl as she sat meowing behind me.

"There you go, Luna. Eat up," I said, patting her gently on the head.

I grabbed a pot and the oatmeal and began making my favorite autumn breakfast: apple and cinnamon oatmeal. Once finished, I sat down at the small dining table and enjoyed my coffee with my breakfast. I was flipping through a magazine and eating breakfast when my phone pinged. I grabbed for my phone and smiled when I saw a message from Peggy; however, reading it wiped the smile off my face.

Peggy: Jenkins ranch has sold.

I stared down at the message, tears coming to my eyes. I had been doing so well without any more tears, until now. I guess it was final. Thomas had gone through with the sale and would be leaving Willow Valley. I had gotten my wish. That my life would go back to normal, only I knew now that wasn't what I wanted at all. I swallowed hard and shoved the half-eaten bowl of oatmeal away from me and hit reply. Through tear-filled eyes, I managed to type, "I know. I don't want to talk about it," and hit send. Then I buried my face in my hands and let it all out, already missing the feeling of his arms wrapped around me as my phone continued to ping.

An hour later, I'd showered and dressed, making my way over to The Crispy Biscuit. It was a quiet morning there, and I walked inside and right up to the counter.

"Good morning, Trinity," Brooke said, wiping her hands on her apron, smiling.

"Morning. Can I get four apple fritters please?" I asked, making sure to avoid eye contact with her.

"Sure thing." She smiled, grabbing a bag from the counter behind her.

The last thing I wanted to do was to be asked about Thomas, and since we had normally gone to having breakfast Sunday mornings here, I figured that would be the first question on her lips.

"We hoped you'd come in today," Melinda said, bringing out a fresh tray of croissants. "Where's Thomas?" she asked, looking around the diner.

"Hi, Melinda," I greeted. "I'm alone today and won't be staying."

"Did you hear the news? Serenity sold the Jenkins

ranch," Melinda said, sliding another tray into the display case. "I drove by on my way in this morning. Sold sign up on the driveway. I didn't even know it had been listed."

Brooke glanced in my direction then turned to Melinda and shook her head and held her finger up to her lips, but Melinda kept talking.

"Oh, and I wanted to apologize for the meal choices that Thomas brought to you last month. I was only having fun. Brooke told me all about what happened between the two of you and how he treated you all those years ago."

"Melinda now really isn't the time," Brooke whispered, looking over at me.

Melinda nodded and turned, heading toward the kitchen.

"I'm sorry about that. Serenity was in this morning and told me the news." Brooke softly smiled. "I can't imagine what you're feeling. I remember how heartbroken you were before."

I stood there, feeling a little shocked on the inside at her apology. I'd always thought Brooke had been after Thomas, and I am sure at one time perhaps she was, which is why our friendship had weakened.

"It's fine, Brooke. Thank you both for looking out for me. I appreciate it." I swallowed hard and grabbed the bag of fritters from Brooke and handed her a twenty. "Keep the change. I'll see you next week."

"They are on the house. You enjoy them. Say hello to Vi for me," Brooke said, refusing to the bill from me.

"Thanks, Brooke."

The drive out to the retirement residence was quiet —just me and the loud, annoying thoughts in my own head of Thomas. I'd turned on the radio, anything to try and drown out my own thoughts. The other night I'd asked him to come and see Aunt Vi with me. I didn't want her worrying about me, and at this moment, I was glad I decided against it. I could only imagine what the tension would be like in this car and throughout the day had he been sitting beside me.

I walked through the halls finally coming to Aunt Vi's room. I glanced in and saw that she was sitting by the window, working on another cross-stitch. I couldn't help but watch her face; the expression was one of pure concentration. As I studied her longer, I worried that it wasn't concentration I saw but pure sadness. I wondered if she was lonely.

"Hey, Aunt Vi!" I called, holding up the bag that held the fritters and dangling it between my fingers.

"Hi, Pet. What is that you brought me?" she asked, looking up at me.

"You know exactly what it is. Those apple fritters from Brooke's bakery. She'd just made a fresh batch this morning, and I knew I had to grab them when I saw them."

"Oh, I figured you would have forgotten," she said, setting aside her cross-stitch and crossing her hands in her lap.

"Wouldn't be like me to forget something that important." I smiled. "Oh, and I brought you something else," I said, reaching into my bag to produce the journal I'd found. I held it out for Aunt Vi to take. "I forgot it the last couple of times I came."

A soft smile came to her lips as she looked down at the journal I held in my hand. I could tell she recognized it instantly. She reached out and took it from my hand, her warm, soft fingers grazing mine. I watched as she ran her fingers over the leather cover, then opened the inside and looked down at the writing. Then she muttered something to herself that I couldn't hear and closed the book, setting it beside her.

"Have a seat, Pet," Aunt Vi said, patting the chair that was across from her.

I slipped out of my sweater and laid it on the back of the chair and then took a seat. "So, are you happy here?" I questioned. "Is everything going okay?"

"Very much so. I've been taking a pottery class, if you can imagine that, and doing gardening. They even had a cooking class. The instructor thinks she knows things, but I tell you, she does most things backwards." She smiled.

I laughed. I could only imagine her taking advice on how to cook from someone like me. I'd never known Aunt Vi to be interested in pottery, so I nodded. "The pottery sounds interesting."

"It is, dear. You should try it. I think you'd be very good at it." She smiled, looking over at me, a serious look lining her face.

"What is it?" I questioned, worried that maybe she was really hating it here and only trying to put my mind at ease that she had made the right decision.

"Trinity, how would you like to go out to the garden?"

"It's pretty cold out, Aunt Vi," I said as I looked out the window at the large gardens that sprawled across the empty fields and took in the other residents who were out walking about.

"That's what sweaters are for, dear."

"Okay, Aunt Vi. Shall I get the nurse to get you a wheelchair?" I asked, wanting her to be comfortable.

"No need. I can still move about, you know. Just because a little arthritis has set in doesn't mean I can't still get up and go on my own."

I smiled and stood, helping Aunt Vi up. I let her lead the way as we made our way out into the gardens. She led me over to what was left over of a small rose garden that had a cement bench in the center, and we both sat down.

"This must be gorgeous when everything is in bloom," I said, taking in what was left of the roses that surrounded us.

"It is. Soon, though, everything will be wrapped up for winter. I love to come out here and sit and think. It's rather peaceful, and the roses are gorgeous. Next summer we will sit out here when you come to visit me."

We both sat there in silence, looking around. I wanted to spill my guts to Aunt Vi, tell her everything that had happened, yet I didn't even know where I was supposed to start. Instead, I decided just to keep it all to myself. I didn't want to upset her. I also didn't want to upset myself, even if I could have used her comfort —the way she'd comforted me the night he'd left the first time.

"What is it, Pet?" Aunt Vi asked as she studied me.

"What is what?"

"Trinity, I've known you all your life. You can't fool me. What is wrong? Is the business in trouble?"

I couldn't help but giggle. "No, Aunt Vi, the business is fine. Booming."

"Well, it's something," she said, bringing her fingers to her lips in deep thought. "A boy perhaps, or should I say a man now?"

I blinked hard. How did she always do this, I wondered.

"You know, Trinity, I fear I may have been wrong all these years."

I frowned. "What do you mean?" I questioned.

"Well, I taught you to just be happy with whatever you had. I also taught you that love wasn't worth it, but without love in the middle…you have no stories to tell, you have no happy ever after either."

I frowned. "Well, Aunt Vi, I'm more of a happily for now kind of girl anyways."

"Trinity, you are only repeating what I've told you for years. I want you to listen to me, Trinity. It's the end that really counts. If the middle leads you to your happily ever after, nothing else truly matters, but without it, you remain empty forever."

Irritation flooded my body. The last thing I wanted to hear was something about some happily ever after. Besides, Aunt Vi wouldn't know anything about that. She hadn't gone after her happily ever after either.

"Aunt Vi, I…"

"No, listen to me. I never told you this. You may know it because you found that journal, so I'm assuming you read it, but years ago I, too, had my heart broken."

"Aunt Vi, really I—"

"*Listen*," Aunt Vi bit out, meeting my eyes with a

stern look, silencing me just like she used to when I was young. "Like you, the man I'd fallen in love with left me. I wanted to die. Really, I did, and in many ways, I think I allowed myself to. I'd gotten pregnant, you see. When he left, I had a miscarriage. I never told Mama, your grandmother, or him. Only your mother knew. Years later, when I was in my late twenties, he came back to Willow Valley. He sought me out, only when I saw him, I pushed him away. I wanted nothing to do with him, and I mean nothing."

Thinking back, I wondered if this was why Thomas had asked me to read the entire journal. I'd never known that Jed had come back to Willow Valley. The only thing I'd found was that letter, and I figured it had come in the mail.

"I was still so hurt, and just looking at him ripped at my heartstrings. He tried to get me to talk to him. He even wrote me a letter and everything, leaving it at the front door with your mother, but the damage had been done, and I decided that it was too late for us. I never wrote him back. Instead, I shoved that letter in that diary and never opened it again. I chose to live a very lonely life. I mean, I had you after your parents passed, so I wasn't completely alone, but it was still lonely, not having anyone to love in the way a woman loves a man. I chose wrong, Trinity."

"Aunt Vi…"

"Trinity, stop being so stubborn. You don't want to end up like me. God is granting you both a second chance with one another. That is a gift that not many people get. You should be grateful. Let the anger go and realize what it is you are being handed. Sometimes, my dear, the road to the happily ever after isn't paved, it's rocky and bumpy, but that is what makes the relationship that much stronger."

I looked at Aunt Vi, my eyes beginning to burn with tears.

"Second chances don't come along often in life. I lost out on so many things because I didn't take the second chance that was being handed to me. I let my anger and hurt get in the way, and the only thing it did was burn me."

I looked down at my hands. They were folded in my lap, and without warning, tears rolled down my cheeks. I looked up at Aunt Vi, and she reached over and wiped them off my cheek.

"Just realize what it is you're being given. Open your heart instead of keeping it in that proverbial locked metal box that I taught you to keep it in," she said, softly smiling.

"But, Aunt Vi, he hurt me again," I whispered.

"That's because you're still allowing what happened in the past to interfere with now. Stop, just stop. Forget what happened and open your heart to the new possibilities. He isn't the same man he was before."

I leaned over and wrapped my arms around her when a deep voice called out from behind us, "Knock, knock."

I turned and looked over my shoulder to see Jed leaning against a walker.

"Jed," we both said at the same time, only the shock that lined my voice didn't line Aunt Vi's.

"I'm not interrupting anything am I."

"No, dear, not at all." Aunt Vi smiled, patting a spot on the bench beside her.

I watched as Jed made his way over and sat down, then leaned in and kissed her cheek. A light blush fell over Aunt Vi's cheeks, and I brought my hand up to cover my smile.

"I thought I'd come to see if you wanted any lunch. They are serving some pasta in the lounge, with some garlic bread. Strawberry rhubarb pie for dessert."

"That sounds delicious. What do you think, Trinity?"

I smiled and nodded. "Sounds really good."

"We'll be right in. Save us a spot," Aunt Vi said and leaned over placing a kiss on Jed's cheek.

Once Jed was gone, Aunt Vi leaned over to me and placed her hand on my knee. She met my eyes and softly smiled. "Seriously, Trinity, it's the end that matters the most. Trust me, and don't wait until it's too late, like I've done. Because of my inability to let go of the past, I now have only a very limited time with him. Now let's go get us some lunch."

"Aunt Vi?"

"Yes, dear?"

"Thanks for the talk, but how do you know about Thomas being back?"

"Because, dear, he came to see me, but he's been talking to Jed a lot this past month. He told me." She winked. "Now let's go."

As Aunt Vi got up, I took one look at the soft smile on her face and realized that she had been able to look past all that had happened over the years, all the words written in her diary. I was happy for her, that she had gotten another chance with the love of her life, and I hoped that they would have a long time together. However, it didn't matter. Things between Thomas and I were non-existent. He had already made up his mind; he was moving, and I, no matter what, would end up alone and unhappy. He could talk to Jed all he wanted, but actions spoke louder than words. I just didn't have the heart to tell her.

CHAPTER 19

Thomas

I'd had to return to Serenity's office later Sunday morning to sign more papers. I walked out of the office, a brown manilla envelope in hand, and headed to my truck. I was going to go over and see Trinity, hoping that the dust had settled enough for her to allow me a chance to explain everything. I didn't care if the dust hadn't settled. I wasn't allowing this to rip us apart. Only when I drove by, I noticed a big, closed sign hanging in the window. Then I remembered that she'd said she was heading out to see Vi today.

I stopped at the corner and let out a breath, then

changed my mind and headed in the direction of the flower shop. Perhaps Peggy would be able to help me. After all, those two seemed to be close.

I walked into the small flower shop and waited while Peggy dealt with the woman at the counter. She was completely undecided at what it was she wanted to order, but Peggy kept her wits about her, making suggestion after suggestion, until the woman finally agreed. Then she paid for her order, nodded in my direction, and left.

"Thomas, what can I help you with?" Peggy asked, coming around from behind the counter.

"Well, I need something that screams I'm sorry."

Peggy smirked and then pushed herself off the counter. "Well, then, I'd say white orchids." She went over to the cooler and pulling out some stems of white orchids.

I nodded, putting my trust into Peggy that she wouldn't lead me astray. I watched as she mixed some white orchids against some greenery, running back and forth to the cooler to grab some other things.

"So what happened?" she asked while she continued arranging something.

"A misunderstanding really."

"I bet. They normally are. Care to tell me about it?"

"Well, I'm sure you know Trinity and I have a

history," I said, sitting down on the stool in front of the counter.

"I did," she said, still concentrating on the work at hand.

"Well, she found out that I was selling my parents' place and she blew up at me. She thinks I was going to leave."

"I see, and were you?" Peggy asked quietly.

I shook my head. "No, but she wouldn't even give me a second to explain." I paused, thinking back to all the time she had given me to explain, only my stupid self couldn't ever seem to find the words. "Okay, that isn't exactly true. Perhaps she did give me time, but somehow, I was at a loss for words."

"Perhaps you, yourself weren't even sure of what your plans were."

I shrugged. "Maybe."

"And now."

"Well, I'm here, right? I know what I want now."

"Do you?" Peggy asked as she tied the white ribbon around the bouquet and then wrapped it up in a pink paper, smiling at the finished product.

"I do." I nodded.

She reached over and grabbed a box of chocolates off her shelf and held them up, gently rocking them back and forth.

I nodded. Trinity used to love chocolate, and I was sure she still did. "Yes, please," I answered.

"Oh, and what about this?" Peggy said coming, around the counter, walking over to the biggest bear I'd ever laid eyes on sitting in the corner. "Trinity has loved this bear since I got it."

I gave her a skeptical look, but her expression was so serious, I knew there was no way I was leaving this shop without it, especially if it meant making Trinity happy. "Okay, no problem, throw that in as well," I replied and reached for my wallet while Peggy quickly tabulated my bill.

Half hour later, I was on my way out to the retirement residence with a giant stuffed bear sitting in the passenger's seat.

CHAPTER 20

Trinity

The dining room was quiet now. Most of the residents had eaten and returned to their day. We still sat there, empty plates in front of us, sipping on coffee.

“That was excellent,” Jed said, placing his arm on the back of Aunt Vi’s chair while I ate the last bite of my pie.

“Sure was,” Aunt Vi agreed.

“So how did you two meet again, after all these years?” I asked.

“Well, if it hadn’t of been for my good friend Thomas, we never would have.”

"Thomas you say?" I questioned, meeting Jed's eyes.

"Yep. He was a lot like me. Left Willow Valley young to chase after a dream. He, too, left behind a young girl, who he loved dearly. I think I remembered seeing him with her once or twice. She was a pretty little thing. I believe her name was Tiffany or Tammy."

"Trinity?" I asked.

Aunt Vi looked over at me and smiled.

Jed looked over at me and smiled. "That is it. Did you know her?" he questioned. "Go to school with her?"

"Jed, this is my Trinity," Aunt Vi answered. "My niece. Thomas's Trinity." Aunt Vi laughed at the look on Jed's face and then looked over to me and winked.

"Aunt Vi, please, don't call me that."

"What a small world," Jed said, winking at me and then looking past me. "And would you look at that, there he is now, my friend Thomas," Jed said, pointing behind me.

I closed my eyes at the sound of his name. He was the last person I'd wanted to see, the hurt from yesterday still too raw. Yet I turned to see Thomas pushing a wheelchair that held the huge bear I recognized instantly from Peggy's store, and almost laughed out loud. One of the nurses walked beside him holding a wrapped bouquet of flowers and a box of chocolates.

"Oh my, look at all that." Aunt Vi giggled and placed her hand on my shoulder. "Remember what I said," she said, meeting my eyes with a stern look.

As Thomas approached the table, he slowed the chair and then thanked the nurse as he took the flowers from her hands. He smiled and nodded at Aunt Vi, greeting Jed before turning to look at me. I couldn't help but meet his eyes. Had he done this for me?

"Trinity, before you say anything…"

"I see that not only did Melinda get you, but it looks like Peggy got you really good as well," I said, looking over the over-sized bear that sat in the wheelchair. I'd remembered when she'd purchased that bear last year. She'd figured it would sell in a heartbeat; however, it had sat in the corner ever since collecting dust.

Thomas grinned. "Nothing is too good for my girl," he said, holding the flowers out for me to take.

I looked at him, then reached for the package and opened the pink paper and smiled down at the white orchids. "These are beautiful," I whispered, tears coming to my eyes as I leaned down so Aunt Vi could see.

"She may have gotten me good, but she was trying to help as well."

"That is wonderful that she cared enough to help, but, Thomas, flowers and a bear isn't going to fix this."

"I know that. However, it's a start though. I want to talk to you, to explain to you that what you're assuming isn't true. I tried the other morning, but you kicked me out."

Aunt Vi looked up at me and gripped my arm. "What happened the other morning?" she asked.

I shook my head and leaned down to whisper in her ear that I'd tell her all about it another time. Then, taking my hand in hers, I stood up and met Thomas's eyes. "Don't push me, Thomas. I'll do it again," I said, holding my ground.

I felt Aunt Vi's hand slip from mine and felt it on my hip instead. I looked down to Aunt Vi, who gave me a look to at least hear him out. "Jed, I think it's time we take a walk," Aunt Vi said, standing up, waiting for Jed. He slowly rose to his feet and grabbed his walker, and together they made their way over to the other side of the room where they sat down with another couple.

"Trinity, one thing I do know is that you can't kick me out of here. You don't own this place." Thomas grinned, looking proud of himself.

I looked up at Thomas and frowned. "Don't bet on it. Besides, I don't know what you could possibly have to say to me. You sold the ranch, and you have nowhere to go, which means you'll be leaving again," I said, covering the flowers back up.

"Trinity, you are so wrong. You won't even listen to why I sold the ranch?"

"Like I said, I already know why."

"No, you think you know why. I sold it because it was flat broke. It would take all my time to try and hopefully bring it up to where it should be, and I can't do that if I want to be with you. I certainly can't do it with this broken body either."

I was about to tell him I told you so, but I stopped as the words he'd spoken sunk in. He'd sold the ranch to be with me? "What?"

"That's right, Trinity. The amount of work that ranch would have required from me to get it up and running to where it should be would have taken all my time. There would have been no chance for us to even try and begin rebuilding what we'd lost. Since I returned to Willow Valley and walked in that bookstore to see you standing there, everything became clear to me. The second I saw you; I knew in my heart that I wanted to be with you, in that small apartment, helping you run that bookstore. Ranching was never in my heart, and I doubt all those years I'd spent in the rodeo never were either. The only thing I do know is that you never left my heart, not for one single second."

My eyes stung with tears at his words. "Why didn't

you ever tell me that?" I questioned, wiping the tears that had begun to fall.

"It's not every day that you spill your guts to someone. If I had walked into that bookstore and said those words, you'd of laughed me right out of there. When I should have said them, I couldn't find the words, and with the way you found out about me selling the ranch, I don't think you would have believed a word I said anyways," Thomas said, stepping closer.

"You might be right," I whispered, stepping into him.

We stood looking at one another. Then he placed his fingers on my chin and lifted my head, bringing my eyes up to his. "Might be right?" he questioned.

"Okay, you are right."

"That's why I told you to read all of your aunt's journal. Jed did come back, and Vi pushed him away. She wrote all about that regret, but you were insistent you knew all about her."

"Yeah, she told me today," I whispered, looking up at him.

"Trinity, I've lived most of my life without you, and it's something that I no longer want to do. I've never stopped loving you, despite what you might think. I want you to be my forever."

I inhaled deeply, fighting back the sob that was stuck in my throat. "Really?"

"Really, Trin. It's not too late for us to find our happily ever after, right here in Willow Valley. Let's not wait some fifty or so years to get a chance."

My body felt heavy at his words, and the sobs started as he pulled me into his arms. My head rested on his strong chest, and when we parted, I closed my eyes as his lips meant mine. When our lips parted, I met his eyes. "Let's do this," I whispered, even though deep down inside I was scared to death.

Thomas wrapped me in his arms and pulled me against him this time, not letting me go. The longer we stood there, the less scared I felt, and a sense of safety and belonging emerged.

"Does this mean you two have decided to give yourselves a second chance?" Jed asked just as Thomas bent to kiss me again.

I pulled away and curled into his side, a happy feeling settling over me.

"Sure looks that way," Thomas said, pulling me in closer.

"Like I said, Trinity, the ending is what counts, so make it count. Both of you," Aunt Vi said, taking hold of Jed's hand.

CHAPTER 21

Trinity
Eight Weeks Later

The past few weeks were busy and filled with many nights of sorting through all the Jenkins' household goods. We had donated a lot of items, while we sold much more, and once the ranch had changed hands, we drove down the driveway of Jenkins Ranch for the last time.

Thomas and I had talked in great deal about him buying his own place or moving in with me. We'd also looked at the option of us buying a place together and making it our own, but soon came to realize that there was no reason for either option. Instead, he moved in with me. We'd rearranged the small apartment over the bookstore, gave it an overhaul, and purchased some new furniture and appliances and were now comfortably set up.

"Oh, I ordered those new shelves for the store," Thomas said over breakfast one morning.

"Great, when will they be in?" I questioned as I scooped another spoon of oatmeal into my bowl.

"The delivery notice said two weeks from today. I'd imagine I'll only need a few hours to get them set up. The store may be a mess for a day or so."

I smiled. "That's not a problem. We can do one shelf at a time. It will help once the addition is finished. We will have more space," I said, excited about the expansion.

It had been something Aunt Vi and I had always talked about, expanding the store. Thomas had finally talked me into it, and we'd hired a contractor to put an addition on the side of the building. While that was going on, Thomas had been working diligently on the list I'd given him when he'd returned to Willow Valley. He'd crossed off almost everything and was now focused on the inside of the store. So far, he'd planned on helping set up the new addition and making me a new counter. Turned out that plan had led to a new venture for Thomas. He had a knack for woodworking and had set up a small shop out in the garage behind the house.

"When do you plan on opening up Jenkins Woodworks?"

Thomas shrugged. "I still have a bunch of things to do to have a successful opening, so I figure that I'll get you all set up first, and then work on everything over the winter. To get the word out, perhaps, we could set up a single shelf in the store to hold some of my things until I am fully open."

"I think we can do that." I smiled, taking a sip of my coffee, excited for the future. When Thomas had approached me with the idea, we talked a great deal about his woodworking shop idea, and I promised I would help him with the business side of it. He'd been hard at work making items over the past couple of weeks, and I knew that with hard work over the coming months, he should have a fully stocked storefront in no time. I couldn't see what was really holding him up.

"What else do you need to do to get ready?" I questioned. "We really should have some sort of a date set aside, that way we can put a notice out in the local paper. You know, once the sign arrives."

Thomas buried his spoon in his oatmeal and leaned back against the chair, meeting my eyes. I had a feeling there was something he wasn't telling me. "I suppose that sounds fine."

I studied his face, the lines of worry carved there. "What is it? Something's got you worried?"

"Nope, it's nothing," he said, placing his hand on mine. "It will be fine. Now about Sunday..."

Sunday morning, Thomas and I drove out to get Aunt Vi and Jed from the home. Then we headed into the city. Aunt Vi and Jed wanted to go to a new restaurant that had opened up—Oceanside Steak House, on the outskirts of Willow Valley.

We'd been seated about half an hour, appetizers sat in the center of the table, and our order had been placed. Aunt Vi had been asking questions about the bookstore, while Thomas and Jed talked about Thomas's woodworking.

I placed my hand on Thomas's and smiled as I listened to him as he agonized over an opening date.

"Trinity thinks I should have a solid date in place. I, on the other hand, want to get everything lined up first."

"I just don't understand why. It's a date. It can

always be moved if something goes wrong. It's just more of something to work towards."

"I agree with Trinity," Aunt Vi said, nodding her head. "You need something to work toward."

Instead of saying anything, Thomas let out a breath.

"Thomas, what is it?" I asked, looking at Aunt Vi and Jed as both of them looked over at me and then over to Thomas, each of them wearing a small smile on their face. "What is it?"

"I wasn't going to say anything," Thomas said, grabbing my hand. "I promised Vi and Jed that we'd make it through the meal first, but what the hell... Besides, they are practically giving it away."

I looked to them both, completely confused about what was going on. "Giving away what?"

Thomas let out a breath and then turned to me. "I was thinking, I don't want to open the business until after February."

"February? Why then? It's so far away."

"Well, we have so much to do over the coming months."

"What do we have to do over the coming months?" I questioned, looking at Thomas and frowning. The remodel on the store was almost finished. All we would have left to do is the counter, and he had just stained that. He said it would go in next week, along with most of the shelves. Plus, the apartment had already been updated. There was nothing left, so I seriously had no idea what it was he was speaking of.

Thomas looked across the way at Jed and Vi then reached into his pocket. "Well, I figure we will just be getting back from our honeymoon then, and before then it wouldn't be the ideal time to start up a new business with all we have to do to plan our wedding."

"What?" My jaw dropped as he held out the tiny jewelry box that held the most beautiful ring. Instantly, I brought my hand to my mouth and looked across the table at Aunt Vi, who sat there smiling holding Jed's hand, then I looked back to Thomas.

"It was my mother's." Thomas smiled, sliding the ring onto my finger.

I bit my bottom lip and looked down to the ring that sat on my finger. It couldn't have fit more perfectly.

He met my eyes, a soft smile on his face. "Yes, so we have to plan a wedding and honeymoon. I was planning to ask you to marry me a little later tonight, but now is as good a time as any."

Shock ran through me at his admission, and I was lost for words as I stared at the ring on my finger.

"What? What is it? Don't you want to marry me?" Thomas asked.

"Don't want to? Are you crazy? Of course, I want to," I cried, jumping into his arms.

"This calls for a huge celebration. Dinner is on Vi and I," Jed said, patting Thomas on the back as he kissed me.

EPILOGUE

Trinity
November 2022

Sunday has become my favorite day. As I look back over the past few months, I realize now that I had been more stubborn than I ever needed to be toward Thomas, but regardless, he stayed, and I will be forever grateful that he returned to Willow Valley this past summer. Peggy tells me not to look at it as being stubborn, but to look at it as being protective of my heart. That is what happens when a person has been hurt; they become afraid to trust again, she says. Whichever it is, it turned out that Thomas wasn't as easily swayed by my stubbornness or protectiveness, nor is he now, which deep down inside I am grateful for.

"What are you thinking about?" Thomas asked as he looked up from his menu. It had become a habit since we'd gotten back together to spend some quality time together on Sunday. So, every Sunday morning, we get up and get dressed and head down to The Crispy Biscuit, then afterwards we take a drive out to the lake.

"Not a thing." I smiled, looking back down at the open menu in front of me.

"I doubt that. You look like you're up to something." Thomas chuckled.

"Who me?" I asked innocently, and laughed.

"What are you going to have?" he questioned.

Our eyes met, and at the same time we both shouted out, "Waffles!" We both broke out into laughter as he reached across and took my hand in his.

"Well, if it isn't Willow Valley's two new love birds," Brooke sang as she approached our table.

"Morning, Brooke," I answered. "The place is looking amazing with all the Christmas decorations. You always decorate this place up so nice," I said, looking around.

"Thanks. It's coming. I just have the two front windows to finish, and then I think we should be all set. Are you doing anything to the bookstore this year?"

I nodded my head. "I always do." I smiled. "Just

not sure yet about what? I have a larger window space now," I said, thinking about how much room the expansion had given me.

"What can I get you two this morning?"

"Waffles for Trin, and I'll have sausage and eggs please. Oh and another cup of coffee," Thomas answered.

We watched as Brooke scribbled our order down on her notepad. "Oh, Thomas, I am going to need a shelf to replace the one our mugs sit on. When you get up and running, do you think you could make me one."

I'd been telling everyone in town about Jenkins Woodworks the second the sign had arrived, and Thomas already had a pile of orders he'd started working on. One thing about small towns, word travels fast, and the best part of Willow Valley is that everyone supports each other.

Thomas looked over at me and shook his head. "Really, Trinity?"

I couldn't help but laugh as I nodded my head, "Really. Now take the lady's order." I winked.

"I'll take measurements before I leave," Thomas answered.

Once Brooke had left the table, I pulled the small wedding planner I'd ordered out of my purse and placed it on the table. Then I opened it up to the catering page and wrote down a pile of foods we would have to order. We were well onto desert by the time our breakfast arrived. Brooke set our plates down as I closed the book and placed it back into my purse.

"Here we are," she said, plopping the bottle of syrup down on the tabletop.

"Oh, what sort of Christmas goodies will you be making this year?" I questioned as I poured syrup onto my waffles. "I am trying to figure out what to take out to Aunt Vi and Jed in the next couple of weeks."

Brooke thought for a moment. "Well, I am trying something new. I made them last week. I just need to tweak the recipe a bit, but I think I am going to call them Soft, Gooey, and Oh so Sticky Cinnamon Buns."

"Those sound freaking delicious. I wish you had them here now." I laughed.

"They were to die for! Seriously!" Brooke said as the little bell above the door jingled. "Enjoy your breakfast. We'll talk in a few," she said, leaving the table to greet a couple who had just walked in.

As we sat across from one another, talking about our wedding and Christmas and the new ventures with Bluebird Books and Jenkins Woodworking, I realized Aunt Vi had been right. The ending was what counted, the happily ever after, but I also think the journey is important to. After all, it is what leads us to that happily ever after. Aunt Vi was right about that as well.

I picked up my coffee and took a sip. Then I smiled at Thomas, and I realized in that moment how grateful I was. Grateful for the memories of the past that brought us back together, and I welcomed the future and all of the memories we were about to make.

Get ready to return to Willow Valley in December with The Holiday Dilemma

Christmas has always been my favorite time of year. My bakery, The Crispy Biscuit, is all decorated and every year I feature a new holiday recipe. This year, it's none other than my soft, gooey, and oh so sticky cinnamon buns. As I'm making the first batch, I sit down to read through my favorite baking magazine only to find out that they are going to be filming their Countdown to Christmas Bake Off event right here in Willow Valley.

I'd entered this contest the last two years, both times coming in second place. Everyone tells me that the third time is a charm and so with the whole town routing for me I enter my cinnamon buns.

The day of the try-outs I arrive with my buns and a smile, only to discover Tristan Ryan sitting on the judge's panel. We went to culinary school together. We didn't have a good relationship then, especially when he voiced that he didn't think I deserved to be at one of the top culinary schools if all I was going to do was take over my mother's bakery back in my small hometown.

There was no way I was going to let him get to me. When my name was called, I raised my head high and climbed up the stairs to the stage. That was when it happened, my ankle went rolling, my rolls went flying, and my mouth…well I started cursing. I'm still not convinced the trip was just an accident.

Tristan claimed the guilt, I guess that's why he stayed. He even moved right into my house beside the bakery. He took care of me and my broken ankle, and even volunteered to help with the bakery. To my surprise, the criticism seemed to stop, and something else started. I was beginning to like the big dumb jerk.

I don't know what I was thinking, a week later, he was itching to go, but promised to stay long enough for the contest. I knew it would never last. After all, Tristan always had a way of testing my patience, and I was convinced he'd decide soon enough there was nothing for him in this little town, including me, so what harm would come from a little fling?

The Holiday Dilemma

Releasing December 13
Preorder Today

ABOUT THE AUTHOR

USA Today Bestselling Author S.L. Sterling was born and raised in southern Ontario. She now lives in Northern Ontario Canada and is married to her best friend and soul mate and their two dogs.

An avid reader all her life, S.L. Sterling dreamt of becoming an author. She decided to give writing a try after one of her favorite authors launched a course on how to write your novel. This course gave her the push she needed to put pen to paper and her debut novel "It Was Always You" was born.

When S.L. Sterling isn't writing or plotting her next novel she can be found curled up with a cup of coffee, blanket and the newest romance novel from one of her favorite authors.

In her spare time, she enjoys camping, hiking, sunny destinations, spending quality time with family and friends and of course reading.

Join my reader group on Facebook
Sterlings Silver Sapphires

Not on social media? Sign up for my newsletter

Visit my Website

OTHER TITLES BY S.L. STERLING

It Was Always You

On A Silent Night

Bad Company

Back to You this Christmas

Fireside Love

Holiday Wishes

Saviour Boy

The Boy Under the Gazebo

The Greatest Gift

Into the Sunset

The Spencer Brooks Diaries

Our Little Secret

Our Little Surprise

The Malone Brother Series

A Kiss Beneath the Stars

In Your Arms

His to Hold

Finding Forever with You

Vegas MMA

Dagger

Doctors of Eastport General

Doctor Desire

All I Want for Christmas (Contemporary Romance Holiday Collection)

Constraint (KB Worlds: Everyday Heroes)

Willow Valley

Memories of the Past

Ingram Content Group UK Ltd.
Milton Keynes UK
UKHW012118060323
418148UK00003B/135